Acknowledgements: Thank you to my loving mom, dad, brother and 2 year old cat. My friends, who have been amazing in helping me push through this process of publishing my first book. And to my therapist, who jokes "you've been trying to publish for years." Well here we are.

Chapter 1:

Chris Stallingworth was his name. He was the man on the news who recently got divorced. He had light, thick brown hair that was about an inch away from the top of his forehead that jutted out in all directions. He was passed out on the street, and some thugs took him away until the police caught them.

What?

Shakes eyes with his hands

Huh?

He got up, in the middle of the city, lost in the bar that was just across from work, where two guys took him out one by one, about to hit him with a bat. That's when the police came and saved him.

"Chris?"

I-it's Chris. Chris Stallingworth. He wanted to say.

Instead, he said, in embarrassment with the beer and dirt drenched all over his body.

"No, no it's not Chris. It's Ben."

"Ben who?"

Thank God no one in his town knew of him beside the neighbors or else the talk of the town would be on him. But he held his composure despite the beer falling from his sweater, the blood that was scraped from his stomach after being dragged, and the tears that were in his eyes.

That night he collapsed on the floor after a quick hospital visit, thinking of nothing else. The thugs were held in custody.

The news outlet, however, was not deceived by the name Ben, knowing who it was.

He turned the television off in disgust and thought. Thought about her.

He reminisced about how they met. She was a thin woman with the face of an angel and deep black hair. She had a soft touch in her eyes and a gentle way she touched him. Nobody knew why she loved him. But she did.

He slammed his fist against the table next to his chair. Then he stopped, and the room was silent. He could have gone to his father's at some point to play chess. That's all he could think of. Yet, here he was.

Days would pass by and people would forget. Forget about his appearance that night. Forget that he was recently divorced. Forget that his childhood dreams of becoming a father all at once were diminished. Diminished because he was divorced.

He stopped for a moment. There was nothing. The wind hollered as much as the screaming of the two men that took him outside, dragging his feet, and the blood that was against his belly. But he didn't feel that, it was more numbing pain. The beer was so tight in his hands when it happened, and then it fell, drastically, like a commercial product falling to the ground. Then, he fell too, his hands becoming scraped. They didn't drag him far, as there was already a police escort to save him from his pathetic stunt. His black shirt, a shirt she bought him, was instantly ruined.

He frequently drank alone, but this was a scene that nobody anticipated. He sat back at the television and laughed at the sixty-second segment, as the police escorted him back to his home after his brief hospital stay, clearly out of sorts. They checked on him and he nodded that he was fine, and he was fine, really, but then once he got home, the faintest smell of her perfume drove him off again and he felt like going back. And get slammed. By two drunk men.

I deserve it.

No, no, Chris you don't. But I do.

He stopped himself, the quiet filling the house. She once had a laughter that was so gentle, as they would joke around about having kids and living such a normal, peaceful life. She would laugh and place her arm against him, calming his senses. His hair was smooth back then, or completely bald sometimes, and he was approaching his mid-thirties, clean-shaven, with a gray shirt and some black jeans. They would hang out with other couples, her doing that same thing, resting her hand between his stomach and his arm, loving the sensation of her husband's muscles.

He shook his head, trying to metaphorically wipe away the dirt in his hair. He stopped. Getting up, he felt sick, but he stopped. Before he could get sick, he took some water and drank it. Breathing in freshness, he calmed down a little.

The wind outside their small two-bedroom house was howling. It was a house that was once so pristine. Literally. He felt the scratches against the house, and it was just like the men, the tormenting squeals outside, begging to enter the home and collapse him once more.

He shook his head.

What will work look like on Monday?

He laughed at himself.

Such a pitiful thought, maybe go back to mom and dad?

He stopped and thought. He and his dad were going to play chess. It's what he said to him once he got divorced, right before. It was something Chris loved as a child. He loved controlling the pieces and the way that they moved in sync. It was predictable. Unlike his days now.

He calmed down a little, sweat dripping down his body now turning cold, and he let out a sigh of relief.

But then came the pain. The pain in his chest came back and that's when he knew he was raw again. The drink was wearing off now, and now, he was back. His head started spinning, thinking of her. Her image, her voice, and her laugh, all came together like her image was plastered on the scratched walls.

He felt sick again. Then he stopped. Thinking of his father.

He quickly went up and showered, thinking of work.

That night the sickness subsided, but the ache in the pit of his stomach was there, and his heart felt like a woven basket that was pulled apart by a sumo wrestler. Somehow, he didn't know how he was going to survive this.

He turned on some soft music on his phone and repeated in his head what his father would tell him.

"Chris, you're worth it. Don't let some girl get to you."

He stopped and thought about his father. How good of a man he was. How he loved his mother, how they did the same things he did with his wife, and the beautiful chain of events was somehow spiraling out of his control. Her laugh, her face, her image…

He stopped. Again, then thought of his father.

"Chris, don't move that knight. My queen is right around the corner, don't you see those moves?"

He honestly couldn't. His father was a Ph.D. in math. Chris himself was more of a partier, getting good grades and working at a major company trying to make a few electronics, especially working with constructing computer and phone parts. He liked to go out with his friends. Or maybe he should say they were *her friends*.

"Play the goddamn Queen, kid."

Then Chris would make a move. His father was stunned.

"How did you do that?"

Chris would smirk a little. "You know I love this game."

"Yeah, you could have won a lot of awards if you put more effort into it."

Chris was always hurt by those sorts of comments. His father has a Ph.D. and being an only child put much more pressure on him to be his father's successor. Now in his mid-thirties, he couldn't do much good for a Ph.D. if he wanted to.

"Yeah, well I am not as talented as my father." Chris would jab back, and wink. His father would belly laugh and then smile.

"That's my boy."

They would chatter while his mom poured lemonade and made them cookies, Italian cookies, Chris's favorite, for them. They would spoil him, knowing that he was the only one.

His mother was someone he wasn't too close to but loved in the sort of way that he and his father could only know. She was quiet and reserved, cooking in the house and tending to every necessity. She cleaned frivolously and worked as an accountant before retiring. They were a family of understanding numbers and facts.

But Chris's ex-wife wasn't.

She was a part of an exclusive political family, her father, being a part of the top political party. She was perfect, she was smart, and she had money.

But that wasn't why Chris fell for her.

One time in college, he was alone. His grades were slipping, and he felt his hands glide over his face. He was crying. Even though it was a beautiful summer day, he was crying alone in nice khaki shorts and a green button-up. Every time he would cry at home, his dad told him to "shut up and stop crying boy!" But she came over and that's how it all started.

"Chris?"

He suddenly looked at her. They were about 18 at the time. They were in the same economics class. He noticed her before and liked her because everyone knew how gorgeous she was, but she tended to be more reserved. He knew that her father was a famous politician and she got some press occasionally, and unlike the other boys in his class, he didn't even want to try with her. He fantasized occasionally. Maybe it was his insecurity or something else, but she was on the list for many of his college buddies even if she wasn't really into that yet. He was sleeping with other women at the time, admittedly.

The reason she was in this economics class was that it was an extra elective for her nursing degree while he was for his major, along with electrical engineering. Her face was angelic and her words were soft-spoken and gentle. They hung onto him like a sweet song from the 1950s.

"Yeah?" He tried to straighten himself, but his words came out like a croak, and he looked down in red, and in embarrassment. She rubbed his shoulder.

"Are you okay?"

"Fine, fine, yeah, just about the grades you know?" He tried to act cool, but he was losing it. If he was kicked out of college, he would surely stop trying in life. He didn't want to let his father down.

They talked. She talked about her father being a famous politician in another state and how they influenced her to be more "real" with people as she put it. He stared at her eyes, round and watery, soft and gentle, and the more he saw her eyes the more he couldn't stop looking. It was like that favorite home-cooked meal that his mom made or some sort of pastry that you could bite into that was soft and fluffy. He melted in her presence and her touch made him tingle.

"Now, don't you think you should go home...I can walk you home."

He nodded vigorously, almost like a child, as this mysterious woman walked him home.

He acted more like a man later, showing off the tattoo that he got under his arm. He calls it his "badass" tattoo that he got. It was a challenge for his buddy when he was a junior in high school to get it. It represented his celebration of life and his way of connecting with the world.

She dug it immediately. She was flustered. He smoothened his brown hair, like a tattoo would win over any innocent-looking girl dying for intimacy.

She stopped and then the roles were reversed.

"I-I should probably get back." She stammered nervously, slowly sliding her nails against his chest, where he told her to touch the tattoo.

"Well, good thing I'm not in the army."

She laughed like she was in an orchestra and he smiled so often, his teeth white with peroxide and his muscles bulging out. His father was once in the army and told him that pansies didn't work out. But Chris did. Every damn day.

"I guess I see the real you." She smiled.

"I guess you did." He said, shaking his wavy brown hair out of his green eyes.

"Well, see you later." She said, smiling a little, and clutching onto her books, she left him in wonderment.

Chris's head was still pounding that night about the memory. He touched his tattoo, the only one since his dad almost kicked him out that night and his mom was quiet as usual, but looking displeased at it. He regretted it immediately. It technically would have been against the law if he didn't lie about his age. He said he was 22 at the time and even went so far as to get a fake license to get it. Also out of state so that no one would know the parlor and the parlor wouldn't know him. He was able to pull it off since he had an older look even at 16 and he said he went on a "getaway with a friend" to deceive his parents. It was hidden under his shirt and thankfully the thugs didn't ruin it, but he still regretted it.

The one bad decision he made in his life. He got away with it. Plus, when it came up, he told people that his parents consented, and no one pressed him about it. Not even his parents.

She liked it.

Then it was the silly reassurance that he did. *Oh well, if she liked it then I can't. Everything that she does, I can't do it.*

He shook his head and almost laughed as the sides of his skin were aching from the men pulling him out of the bar. There were some slight scars near where his tattoo was.

Nothing she likes I can like.

He sat there in the television room, leaning his head back against the chair, avoiding the bed area where her perfume still lingered, thinking that he'd need some real good steroids to get through work next week. It was only Sunday tomorrow so he'd luckily have time to rest in bed. But he still didn't like himself.

Nothing she likes I can like, nothing she likes I can like, nothing she likes I can-

He kept repeating it in his head. And like that, almost as if the words replaced counting sheep at night, he was out cold in the chair.

Chapter 2:

Chris's stubble was growing out slightly. He looked at himself in curiosity. She always liked the short stubbles, never the full thing. Like either a goatee or a beard. *It was too much, not enough face.*

Her dad was a clean-shaven politician, an almost famous senator from the South, and he had always been clean-shaven, with stark black hair like his daughter's. Chris never knew about who she was until people talked. Chris had to make sure the father respected him. Chris, when he was younger, naively told him about his worthy accomplishments, being in many honor societies.

"Oh there was the honor society I was in…" Chris blabbed about his high school honors society, making it seem like the largest accomplishment he ever had serving in it. The father laughed callously often about it as if he could read Chris's mind. Chris ignored it, always laughing with the father, who seemed to have a new haircut every week, especially when he was on television.

Also with a rigid face and quick sense of humor, Chris's father always had an opinion.

"I don't know if I like that guy, Chris." He rolled his eyes. "You know how politicians are."

"It's fine," Chris said, almost giddy as he was seeing the politician's daughter tonight. That was the only reason he put up with the crap his father gave him. He genuinely wanted to see her.

"You seem too happy."

Chris's mother in their modest home placed the turkey sandwiches on the table. Chris dug in immediately.

"For Christ's sake, answer me, boy."

"Let's say I am happy." He said with food stuffed in his mouth.

His dad rolled his eyes again.

"He's happy, don't you like that?" His mother said in a hushed tone. "He's happy."

"I don't care if he's happy." The father remarked. "If he's marrying a family with trade secrets and fancy smiles, I don't know if he'll be happy later."

"Dad." Chris shook his head and put his hand on his dad's shoulder.

"It's fine."

His dad looked at his mom and nodded.

"Okay, whatever you say."

Chris dressed to impress, much to his parent's dismay, as he wore a bright red shirt and a black tie for his friend's high school reunion party and he was bringing his new girlfriend. He bought the shirt himself.

"Wow, what a stunner." His mother kissed his newly shaven cheek. "Go knock them out."

Chris's dad again rolled his eyes. "Well, have fun."

Then he laughed slightly. "You look good, son."

Chris beamed with excitement, as he took the car out that night. He was anxious, but he bought new clothes and was ready for a real party. Nothing like the lower-class parties that he went to where men walked around in flannels and fires and drank low-class beer.

He drove out, listening to some pump-up music, and noticed the sweat drip down his back. He applied some more cologne on his back and relaxed his shoulders as his head laid heavy against the seat in the passenger seat. He had never done anything really serious with this girl and this was their first night out without her parents. He was playing the 1950 card a few times, making sure that she got home and never tried anything too serious. They have only really gone out a few times. He tried to relax. Something about the night made it seem like *tonight was the night*. Maybe when he took her home. He would take the night to do something more, in a more intimate setting. He was bad, but *that's how men thought*. Looking back on it, he would seriously regret what happened that night.

He finally calmed himself and drove the car. The lights were a little blurred and he passed a few houses. A few neighbors that he knew were inside, as the night was approaching the sun-pressed sky and sky was a dark blue. He stopped on the side of the road and sprayed another shot of cologne on his backside, and he continued to drive forward.

He was close and then saw her waiting for him on the porch. She was dressed in all white in a long dress with a black cover-up. Her silky and shining black hair was tied back with prime red lipstick and a fierce smile. He was sweating even more. She was beautiful, but this also felt a little different.

He sighed and looked at her, knowing that this might not be what he thought.

She smiled at him and relaxed, getting into the car, and then to his dismay, leaned over to kiss him on the mouth.

"I like the red." She whispered under her breath. She put a mint in her mouth before he had picked her up and her teeth were white as pearls.

But there was a hint of alcohol.

He stopped for a moment, thinking about the night he showed her the tattoo. This was a new woman in his car. She almost seemed a little bit aware of his struggles with life in terms of expressing himself, and it's like they switched roles again. He was sure of why she was so confident, but he was feeling all over his body a chilling but tingly feeling.

He put his hand gingerly in hers in the car and they drove, almost in silence, as she leaned a little on his shoulder. It was the alcohol because she was usually a lot shier, but they usually did talk more than this.

"So..." He started, but she was moving her fingers a little more.

"So what?" She smiled a little. "Oh."

"Have you been...um?"

"Drinking?" She smiled. "I took some of my dad's rum in the closet and brought it to your friend's house."

For some reason, he was uncomfortable with it. Like she had a secret side to her that he didn't know about.

He brushed it off. *She's just a little tipsy.*

He continued to talk to her. About her father, about her new internship at a local hospital (she wasn't going to follow in her father's footsteps into politics). They talked about the news, and how her father came home late from his apparent meeting in the statehouse. How he was running for senator and at that time, he had won recently. It was all over the news. She was much more prominent in her state since they lived in a different state than Chris, but she was living with Chris's nearby female friend since they weren't quite at an age where Chris and his girlfriend could live together. Her family let her do what she wanted, and of course the friend, well let's say she let Chris and his girlfriend do whatever they needed.

He remembered his female friend looking shocked when he told her.

"Chris, you know that's the senator's daughter right." Her light brown hair wisped away as they walked down the park where the nearby town garden was.

"Yeah, I know, but she's perfect."

"That's fine, I mean you want her to stay here?" Her green eyes grew a little.

"Yeah, why not?"

She shook her head. "Chris, you can't make her stay here. What is her father going to say?"

The next day she asked if she could stay there and his friend was all for it.

"I am *going to have the senator's daughter over. Holy shit.*"

Chris laughed at her sense of humor. She was a lot like him, a more down-to-earth type of personality with a smug smile and more of a tomboy in her youth. She was not really into dating at that age, but his dad always joked about them together.

"You and our neighbor, ever going to go over there and do more than talk?" His dad smirked at him and gave him quite a disgusted look when he was younger as she would hang out around his guy buddy friends at the local baseball game.

"*Honey,*" his mother said with a rare hiss. "Stop giving him ideas. And she's a fine young woman."

Chris laughed a little and rubbed his mom's shoulder. "Don't worry ma, I'm not doing anything with her."

They were like best friends, ever since they were children. She wasn't Chris's type.

As he was driving he remembered his friend saying that. But it felt right, having the senator's daughter leaning against him. He kissed her forehead slightly and rubbed her leg a little with his arm.

They got to the party a little early. It was a high school reunion formal with a few of his buddies in town. They also thought about trying to organize a dance together.

"I've always loved dancing," she said, her red lipstick driving Chris crazy. She was a free spirit and he loved it.

"I know you have." He said, taking her hands. "Let's dance."

They were on the dance floor that night, taking a few hits and she leaned on his shoulder, but they never really kissed that deeply until that night when she took initiative in his car. He wasn't expecting it. At all.

People murmured as they came into the formal early, joking when he and his girl would "get married." She laughed and patted his arm. "When the time is right."

Chris laughed a little and told them to shut up. There were only a few of them, and she saw the other girlfriends and went over to chat with them.

"Dude," His friend came up to him. "*How'd you get a girl like that?*"

"Dude." Chris was a bit crass with his friend, usually joking, but tonight didn't seem like the night.

"It was the tattoo." He said flatly, shrugging.

"OOOOOH," The boys shouted and pulled him aside as they forced him to chug some of the alcohol that was in the back of the formal.

Chris spit out some of it and then hid in the bathroom, praying that he would be fine and they wouldn't notice his low tolerance. The dance music began and people were more sullen and quiet.

He stepped out and his girlfriend, the senator's daughter, was there. She looked like she wasn't drinking much either. Or at least that is what Chris thought.

"What is with these guys?" She asked, and her question stung Chris since they were high school buddies. He knew them well.

"I know, I know." He said, shaking his head. "They usually aren't this rowdy."

She put her arm around his shoulder and kissed him *again.*

"It's okay, as long as I am with you." She said sweetly.

His heart melted a little. Her shyness faded, and drinking alcohol for her breath was filled with more than he had anticipated.

"You know, why don't we go home?" He offered, thinking about what was on his mind. He wanted to do it, as it would be his first time.

But then he thought again. *She's so innocent. I can't do this to her, not yet.*

She swung around him.

"Come on, let's get out of here." She smiled, almost like she was trying to hide her distaste.

He led the way and then he stopped and kissed her.

"Shall we."

She smiled smugly. "We shall, my knight."

He laughed a little. He liked that reference.

He again drove her home.

"How do you like my friend? Do you like staying with her?"

"She's fine." She replied, tidying up her dress a little.

"Okay, just making sure."

She leaned against him again. "You don't have to make sure for me honey."

Then once they got home, it was Chris's grown-up college fantasies coming to life.

She tugged at his hair and they tangled against each other, so passionate and so in love, the senator's squeaky clean daughter, Chris Stallingworth, the rogue outsider from the main South, squeaky clean South.

Then they heard a knock on Chris's door.

"Wha-

To his daughter's dismay, there was her father, cameras surrounding the car.

Chapter 3:

Chris looked deep into his own eyes. They were green, like grass pastures when shown under a light. Sad and solemn. He turned around and shouted at the mirror. The wind was howling and it was deadly cold outside.

"You're not good enough!" He yelled at himself.

He wanted to break the mirror, but instead softly pounded the bathroom sink. He covered his green eyes and a few tears fell from his cheeks.

His dad was calling him multiple times, but he didn't answer. The house that was once filled with so much hope was quiet and dark. Chris didn't bother turning on the lights.

That night where he lived out only a little bit of fantasy was only memorable because that's when the cameras were in his face. The first time.

"Is that *your daughter* in there?" The reporter near the car asked gleefully, getting a juicy story was the only thing they were interested in.

"Sure seems like it." The politician said sternly with his face scrunched and his head focused completely on the black tint of Chris's car. And it was late at night at that point.

Chris quickly whispered to his girlfriend to hide as he stepped back out, ruffling his red shirt out and letting her fix his hair as he quickly got out on the other side.

"Chris," the politician said crassly. "Where is my daughter?"

"S-she's um-

"Where is she?!" He almost shouted, trying to calm himself. They were on the news, as the cameras were taking pictures and flashing the next day on the news.

"I'll have her for you tomorrow." Chris tried to look more genuine but was freaking out.

"I want her now. She says that she was with you and I tried calling her and she hasn't picked up."

"I-I know where she is." Chris stammered. "She isn't here."

"Then where is she?"

"Back at the party."

The politician looked incredibly displeased like she had just jumped into a pile of poop and wasn't going to come out.

"*What party?*"

"I-I'll get her sir."

"You better. Bring her back here. I'll be waiting."

"O-okay, sure thing." Chris did a thumbs up and went back in the car, speeding as fast as he could.

His girlfriend was in the back sobbing.

"I am so sorry," Chris said lovingly, holding her hand behind the back window.

"*You?*" She sobbed, at the bottom of the seats. "*He's* the one who should be sorry."

The cameras were not following them to Chris's relief.

"Look, we're just going to have to get through tonight."

He pulled up behind the party room, where no one could see them, and she got up in his arms. At that moment, he knew that she would be his wife. He could feel it, just in her gentle eyes looking deep into his.

She kissed him and fell into his arms like a lock into a key.

"Please don't in any way leave me with that monster."

It shocked Chris when she said those words. He tried to not cry as he was close to his father deeply and this was a girl who had to constantly pretend. She was never the one that he thought she was, but she was crying and then immediately put her fingers through his hair.

"This is where you tell me you like my tattoo."

He laughed so hard, so deeply like he was falling even more in love with her.

"You don't have one."

She laughed too, like an angel, and then they got in the car, trying to look as somber as possible.

Chris slammed his fist even more against the kitchen sink the more he thought about the memory.

They went back hand in hand to her father.

She got out, and as tactfully as possible went up to him. The cameras were surrounding them.

She went up and hugged the politician. As awkward as awkward could be.

"I'm doing okay, you don't have to worry." She said shooting Chris a look.

He was shocked at how quickly she could act at the moment.

"Oh honey, I'm just happy you're *okay*." Her father also shot Chris a look.

"Well, Chris. I'm sorry about that altercation." Her father said, shaking Chris's hand as if nothing had happened.

"Let's have her home now, okay? *Where her parents live.*"

Chris vigorously shook his head. "Yes, yes sir."

"How about you come to us sometimes okay?"

Chris shook his head up and down again.

The politician released his daughter and apologized to the cameras. "Just a worried father, nothing to see."

The cameras were pointing to him again, ignoring the request. "How did you win the race as a senator against such high competition?"

"How could you let your daughter go off so easily?"

"She's 18." He replied promptly. "She can do what she wants."

"But-

"That's all the time I have for today. End the production." The politician said in his fancy suit and asked privately to speak to his daughter.

"Look, if I can't talk to my daughter, then please go."

They listened to him and moved away, as the limousine came and was about to take him and his daughter away.

"Thank you, Chris," she hugged him and they went off, not even smiling or waving to Chris after they left. He thought, dead at that moment, that he would never see her again. Unfortunately for him, and even then he wasn't as deeply in love as he got to, he would fall even further in love and stay with her.

The next day, the wind was howling, similarly to how it was that night he was alone, and he played chess with his dad.

"You say *this guy* tried to steal his daughter away from you?"

Chris kept his head down, as he put his rumpled red shirt away and simply wore jeans and a tee shirt.

"Yeah."

His father shook his head. "You need to get this girl out of your life."

Chris was too distraught to be upset, as he was lucky that the news didn't put a special on-air, deeming the altercation as just a simple daughter-dad moment. Although he *was* on the news and the internet as he was dating the politician's daughter.

"Jeez, Chris." Chris's dad put his hand on Chris's shoulder. "I had no idea how prestigious your university was."

Chris released himself. "And what does that mean?"

"I just didn't know you would run into these types of people-

"*What type of people*?" Chris retorted back.

"Well, you know-

"Stop it." His mother came into the room, sneering at Chris's father. "Just stop it."

"What?" Chris's father shrugged. "It's the truth."

Chris went up to his room for a moment and sighed, then came back to his dad, who was eating and talking to his mother.

"Ready to play again?" Chris's father asked Chris.

"As long as *you* don't say something stupid." Chris's mother sneered again.

"What? You were pleasant a while ago."

His mother rolled her eyes and motioned Chris to sit down, which Chris slowly did. They moved the pieces, as Chris wondered if his girlfriend would be impressed with his chess playing. Or that they too could play. He didn't tell her as he would have felt embarrassed with it.

His father was especially focused, moving his knight to the right spot, but Chris didn't see the trap and fell for it, moving his queen promptly to the spot.

"Really?" His dad remarked.

"What?"

"You sure you want to do that-

His dad gleefully moved his queen, taking out Chris's queen and putting him in a spot for checkmate. He usually lost to Chris.

Chris looked down in dismay, and quickly left the seat, his mother worried about him. He went up to his bedroom breathing heavily, and he felt like crying again.

He lifted his shirt up. The letters were blaring back at him. It was a bearcat on the right side of his ribs with trees surrounding the words which said "only the strongest survived."

He put his shirt back down and relaxed slightly. He didn't cry, he just stared at the wall until the sun went down and he fell asleep.

Chapter 4:

Chris wiped some water around his face and looked at himself again. He quickly put some water around his wound coverings, looking foolish as the water dripped to the side. He was manic, in hysteria, and could not calm down. He fell to the floor. His life was slowly falling apart.

She had left only a few days ago, but she still was fresh in his mind. He leaned against the bathroom wall and started to sob quietly.

They didn't have many neighbors even though she wanted to live in the city close to her father, he had done enough damage already, and she finally agreed a small house near her father's large mansion would work out well. He shook his head.

The water dampened his wounds. The hospital was kind to him, touching his sides and making sure he was okay. He was saying her name as they put the cloth on his wounds. They said he may have damaged his ribs and needed to rest.

"Is she here? Please, she's a nurse."

They looked at him, bewildered.

"He's still drunk."

His father left a voicemail saying that he was coming to Chris's house. Chris didn't answer anything, so he didn't know that he was coming.

The door knocked a few times. Chris didn't know who it was, so he quietly went down to his room and took his nearest weapon, and pointed it at the door.

He unlocked it and thrust it forward until he recognized a familiar face.

"Dad?"

"Yes-yes it's me…" He shook a little outside the house. "Can you put the pistol down please?"

Chris had gotten it a long time ago. He never knew who would come to the door. They were somewhat isolated.

"Yes, I can." Chris was so distraught that laughing at that moment would be tragically comical but he decided to not do it.

He put the pistol to the side and let his Dad inside. He was not laughing.

"What the hell boy?"

Chris stared down at his feet, looking ashamed like he would have been when he was younger.

"Turn the lights on, boy." Chris's father looked at his son, clearly concerned.

Chris turned on the lights and revealed the sorry state he was in.

"What is that smell? Is that alcohol?"

His dad meandered into the kitchen and saw the bottles of beer that were piled upon each other in the kitchen sink. Then he immediately saw the scratches on Chris's side and panicked.

"What the hell, Chris."

He lifted his son's shirt and gasped. The local news in Chris's town clearly did not show his parents what was going on.

He fell and started crying in his father's arms. His father didn't say a word and hugged his son.

They stopped and stared at each other, Chris's face red and heavy. He shook his head and went into the living room. His and his ex-wife's house was a two-story house with two bedrooms. They used to have guests until they started sleeping separately. She came home one night with a man holding her hand, to Chris's dismay. She eventually filed after the two of them became a thing. Chris drank and she left as the piles of alcohol filled the house.

His father looked at him, as he knew that Chris slowly wasn't liking his job, slowly he and his wife were pulling away as the money was tight and the men were plentiful, especially a doctor from work.

He was tall and handsome like Chris but with pale skin, black hair, and a witty smile. He had called her "sweetheart," and ignored her wedding ring apparently, according to Chris's lawyer.

How did the lawyer know? He asked a few of the nurses that worked with Chris's ex-wife to get any more details about the divorce. Slowly but surely Chris was out with some friends at work and he drank so often that his ex-wife avoided him heavily, even though they were together while he drank. He slowly opened the door to see the two of them on the stairs looking like deers in the headlights as he was in shambles.

She slowly came up to him and explained to Chris that she filed and told him why. The politician liked this new man. He had a fancy house. He gave her everything she ever wanted. He liked the same things she liked, and just like that after a month of her and Chris staying at the house, she left for the doctor, calling the doctor her "true soulmate," crying at every word.

Chris knew that she loved Chris more. He knew that it was the politician. She was crying one night explaining to her father about some "doctor." Chris remembered before they went to bed that night joking the morning before about having "kids." The politician was suggesting to leave Chris. Chris didn't take it seriously, asking her if she was serious. She brushed it off.

The politician was still on the phone, calling his daughter saying that the doctor would be a "level up."

Chris cringed as he heard that. He and his wife were struggling financially and their house payments were getting larger and larger because they didn't settle for a flat rate, stupidly. They would sometimes fight about how to save, as Chris's alcohol addiction was getting stronger. They didn't have as many friends, but they enjoyed talking about kids.

They frequently talked about having kids, though nothing came about it. The pregnancy tests were always negative and Chris wondered if his wife purposely sabotaged her chances of getting pregnant. He knew that was ridiculous to think about, but it was possible.

Chris stopped crying and his father shook his head.

"I am so sorry Chris. Why don't you come home?"

"What would I do with the house?"

"Sell it."

"Dad."

Chris was sobbing hard and fell against the wall. He couldn't sell the house. *Where would I live? I am such an idiot.*

Those words spiraled in his head. He would be in his mid-thirties childless with no friends and no wife. His job was nearby so he would have to leave his job. His head was spinning again.

His dad put his hand on his son's knee. "Let's get out of here for a while. Call out of work. Let's fly home. Play chess like we used to. I am sure your mom would love to have you home."

Then his dad added. "So what happened at the bar anyways? I am too shocked to remember what you said."

Chris shook his head and told him. Repeated the whole story.

"I went to the bar." He started. "Got some good beer and then just said 'fuck it.' I had no life so I thought maybe I would drink this weekend. Not a doctor for sure. Just fucking making the same electronics. Over and over again. So I went and I drank at the bar. These guys came up to me and I was like 'fuck it again. I didn't think they would beat me up, but they asked about my name and then called me 'Stallingworth.' They wanted my wallet, but I kept it tight. The city here is dangerous. The police came before they could take it but they beat my sides waiting for me to give it to them. They dragged me out, but I was lucky the cops were there. I bet my ass God was there."

Chris stopped crying. "I was lucky as hell."

His dad looked back at him with so much love. He never wanted his son to go through this ever again.

"C'mon son, let's go home."

Chapter 5:

Chris called in for a family emergency as an excuse to leave work and even though it was somewhat frowned upon since he took some vacation already, they granted him two weeks. Sometimes, he would skip work for no great reason other than to watch television, rest, and further his addiction. He eventually stopped taking a vacation at all because he was dedicated to keeping his job. He and his wife had struggled earlier on putting too much pressure on him.

"You're for sex, but this job? Are you focused?" His then-wife worried as he was kissing her all over.

"I am not thinking of it." His face was looking like it was high on drugs.

"Stop it, Chris, seriously. You have to go to work." She stopped suddenly and then rubbed his clean-shaven head.

"I love you, but you have to focus."

He stopped and quickly got his work khakis on and that black shirt she got him for his birthday. He realized how lucky he was to have a girlfriend, rather at that point a wife, like this. People talked about how lucky he was, and how he could get into politics, although it would be incredibly awkward because he was not from the same political party as his father, and it was also awkward when he asked for the politician's blessing to marry his current wife.

"I want to marry her." He said to the politician.

The politician looked unnerved, but he eventually gave in. "Well, you seem to make her happy Chris."

That seemed too easy. He knew all along. The benefits of having a house nearby and the eventual divorce. She could make major money if he screwed up pending a pre-nuptial or if she found someone better. He knew intuitively it was a setup.

But she and he went to a couple's dinners with prestigious politician sons and daughters, rich people of all kinds, and they laughed like they were forever, him and her. They took boatloads of vacation.

Their wedding was in the tropics surrounded by his high school buddies, some college mates, and her friends from college. Her dad spent what seemed like a fortune and his scrunched face around the rowdy boys was telling but he clapped after they said their vows and kissed. She was happy, and therefore, he had to be happy.

She looked deeply into Chris's eyes that day, and in his dismay, she began to cry, almost like she was terrified of the future. But maybe she convinced herself that she could not love anybody else like this man in front of her.

He felt the same. She was so beautiful in white, and her father had taken her up to the altar. It was a pretty standard wedding, except the cameras were there. Her dad had stopped being a senator at that point, somewhat still in the news that he now was looking to either run for mayor of the major city in their state or president. Their wedding was covered with cameras, and Chris's dad was completely flattered. Chris's mom, however, looked like she was struck by lightning.

"This is quite a wedding," was all she could mutter to Chris's father.

"Yeah, but look at how much our son is going to inherit! The cameras, the press! Maybe he'll get in this, you know?" Chris's father said, completely bedazzled by the experience that his logic was out the window.

Chris's mother slightly slapped Chris's father's arm. Chris was in too much bliss to ever wonder if his mother's caution was wise.

Chris took his new wife through their honeymoon, and that's when it started to get more distant. He was in his late twenties, enjoying every minute with her, but something with her seemed off.

"Let's make sure we live near my father," she said in between kisses.

Chris shrugged. "That's fine."

She pulled away and looked out into the ocean. Chris stopped and looked out with her, a fully funded vacation by her father. Some of their trips were on the news, and Chris was all but unsatisfied with the trip. It was his dream, all coming true.

He told his dad previously that he was excited to welcome new kids into the world.

"Yeah, I may name them Brady, after my grandfather, and another son Ben. I just like the name Ben..." Chris went on and on about trying to test to have sons. He was focused on himself.

His wife pulled away slowly and then looked more outside. Chris looked a little worried after that.

"Honey, what's wrong?" He asked her, as she pulled away slightly, and put her hair behind her ear.

She stopped and added. "Nothing, it's okay."

That day they stayed in and watched television. Chris was on his side wondering what happened. She was on the phone with her father the whole day and then she came back and cuddled with Chris. Chris then got irritated.

"Why are you talking to your father on our honeymoon?"

"I am just trying to update him." She said solemnly.

"Look, I love you and I wanted to marry you," Chris said. "Remember I took you to your favorite place, here for our honeymoon, just a *year ago*. Remember the surprise seafood that we got and then I was able to propose to you when you thought that we were visiting your father out here, and I have no idea why we thought that."

She laughed a little at that statement, as Chris's humor and lies always helped her.

"Yeah, why would my father be out here?"

"Exactly my point," Chris said matter of fact. "Why would he be out here? Why would he be anywhere? *I am out here*, and I am for you."

She eventually dropped the phone and slid into Chris's arms while they were watching the local news and then she turned around and kissed him.

"Why don't we do something wild?"

He smiled. She was back to reality.

"And what would that be?"

"Go to the local grass skirt party. I saw signs about it earlier."

He laughed a little. "Isn't it-

"C'mon Chris Stallingworth." She said smugly as her eyes widened. "For me?"

He smiled. He loved this side of her, the innocent yet tauntingly catty woman that he married and fell in love with years ago.

"Alright- where are we going to get our 'skirts'?" Chris asked giddily.

She laughed. "*They're everywhere.*"

Chris tickled her and they fell into the bed, one of the few happy moments they would have together.

They got up and used the rental car to buy garb for the night. Chris and his now wife were laughing together and almost tackling each other as they rushed to get the proper amount of garb together. She was laughing her angelic laugh and he was there, almost like a movie scene where the ending cuts out with the two heroes breaking out in song and the credits come. It seemed like Chris and his wife had been through everything together.

Unfortunately, it was not the end.

Chris bought his stuff and then she put hers through the self-scan and they left together hand in hand.

They went back to the hotel they were staying in and changed into what seemed like barbarians. He laughed at their style. His was more commonplace: just a grass skirt and a tiny shirt along with a flower crown and some paint over his cheeks. She, on the other

hand, had the same type of wear on, but she had gotten plenty of gold and jewelry and looked like *the* queen of the barbarians. He commented that she did, and she laughed so loud that it was like the chandeliers at the fancy hotel they were staying at were going to fall to the ceiling.

They showed up at the party, and there were plenty of more well-off people there. She said that her dad mentioned it earlier, and that's when Chris became more apprehensive.

"Why did your dad suggest this? I thought you said you saw signs."

"He's in the know with a lot of these places because he visits the politicians here." She muttered.

"Look." He said as he turned to her. "I love you, but you've gotta stop with-

"Look!" She pointed to the receptionist. "They're letting us in *for free.*"

Chris almost gave up and sighed with a shrug. They walked inside and that's when the DJ started getting pumped up. They danced and talked to some other couples, saying that they were recently married and on their honeymoon. The news was even there and captured Chris and his new beautifully dressed wife with a few shots.

Chris was ashamed and upset. *Is this just a publicity stunt?*

He wiped his clean-shaven face and hair. He hated the fact he was almost bald, like his wife's father at that point no longer having his bushy crew cut. Chris often kept a more shaggy look, but his wife liked the crew, almost looking like some sort of stuck-up pilot or comical character.

She was leaning on him once they got inside and for a moment, Chris felt a warmth inside of him.

This was the right decision.

But every part of him was also screaming. *Why the hell are we here on our honeymoon when we could be cuddled up watching a movie?*

They welcomed some friends of the politicians, and she and Chris started dancing until there was an unfamiliar male who came up to them. He was big and he brought Chris's wife aside to talk. Chris was not happy about it.

"Hey, this is my wife?"

"Buddy," the big guy said. "Calm down, we're friends, okay?"

He sighed as he then looked over at the other girls. But he couldn't see anyone but his wife, there dancing. He felt isolated, alone, in his corner. The music was loud and was piercing his ears. It was only his karma that affected him at that moment that he realized what it was like so many years ago when his wife didn't fancy anything that his high school buddies were doing.

But this was different. This was their honeymoon.

He put his hands in his pockets and felt up towards his tattoo. He got it when he was younger, around his high school buddies, and they laughed at him.

"Chris, you can't drink that booze."

"Chris, what are you doing with a pretty lady like that?"

"Chris, who do you think you are?"

"Chris stop being a girl."

He stopped at that moment, realizing in his texts, that the hero of the story always conquered his demons, and always came out on top.

He then stopped. It was all in his head. His once bushy, natural head.

He loved bearcats. They were common in the area that he wanted to travel to. So when he headed into the parlor that day, he told his buddies he was getting a tattoo.

In his head, "Damn dude, you're a man. You're going to do this."

But in reality, his friends cautioned him against it.

"I mean, it'll look cool Chris if that's what you want." One of his friends said. "But also you're too young, man."

"I would worry about that at this age." His friend who kept his wife at her house said.

"You're only in high school. What if you get some sort of disease? Plus, aren't you too young to do that now? Why not get it later?"

He did it anyway. Screw everyone.

The tattoo artist punctured right away when he showed them the design. It was a straight shot. He was only 16 when he got it. Not many people got tattoos, especially "educated" people, as the politician would say around him. But he wanted it. It was his birthright. And he did everything he could to get it.

It came out beautifully. The bearcat was menacing and the letters "only the strongest survived" were carved out perfectly on his body. The moment of joy appeared strongly when his friends drank booze in the back of a Southern truck with the "flashing bugs" they called them and the fresh Southern air filling the vicinity.

He remembered the moon and the peace that came with being around there. The air was crisp, he was with his buddies, and the mood was right. He breathed in the air slowly. There were no expectations, just the annoyance of his parents worried about him coming home, but there were no responsibilities, just the freedom of being out in the open. No politicians, no screaming, no crying, no cameras, no real threat of the booze. Just the air and his buddies.

He remembered a conversation he had with one of his buddies while he was holding a beer. They were talking about girls at the school, and they looked through the yearbook, noticing the little idiosyncrasies of each. He was a special friend because he noticed Chris looking at a girl specifically. Someone who looked a lot like his present wife.

His friend held onto his hand slightly and then stopped.

"Dude, whatever girl you marry, make sure it's a good one. You don't want to get divorced."

Chris stopped and thought about it.

His friend went on to talk about how his family was dealing with a divorce, but Chris stopped and shook off the notion. He just felt the breeze. All the girls were beautiful.

He didn't listen when he was younger. Whatever he was going to marry, he knew that it would work out. He didn't think of it. He didn't want to.

Chris felt his tattoo that night and leaned his head back and breathed in the fresh air. His friend was continuing to talk, but he blocked it out.

Only the strongest survived.

He stopped and then got up from the truck.

"Time to go home, boys."

He thought about that memory, as he looked at his wife, talking to this strange man.

There were people everywhere, him in his silly skirt and faux beach scene with his wife talking and rubbing the large guy's arm. That's when he lost it.

"Hey! That's my wife."

The guy stopped him and his wife looked at Chris in shock.

"Chris?" His wife looked back with wide eyes.

"Look," He said to the man, "What are you doing?"

The man stopped for a moment and looked at his wife like Chris was some lunatic off the street.

She smiled so cringeworthy and took Chris aside.

"What the hell are you *doing*?" She hissed at him.

"Who is that guy?" Chris demanded.

"It's none of your business *who he is*." She said, "He's just a friend of my dad. We come here a lot."

Then she added, "I thought you knew that."

He shook his head. "When you said tropical island, you made it seem like you didn't come here often."

She looked forward, "Why don't you talk to some people here, Chris? Get out of your head."

His veins were starting to pop out of his head. "I want to go home."

"Then, go!" She said, "there's the door!"

"I don't want to go." He clenched his teeth.

The room was silent as pairs of eyes were on them. She started crying.

Chris felt awful at that moment.

"Oh, no I'm sorry, babe-

"Look, I have to go," She said, going to the bathroom.

His head was spinning. Spinning with the thoughts of all those pairs of eyes laughing at him. All those pairs of eyes looking up and down like that man did. All those eyes calling him a loser.

"Stop!" He said to himself. "Just stop."

"Is that man okay?" One of the women asked the other one, clearly audible to Chris.

He left to chase after his wife and the silence continued until the party resumed as if nothing happened.

She was continuing to cry in the bathroom when he got there, multiple men were talking to her. Chris's head was spinning, and he just stopped and looked at all the people there. Their faces were blurred, all fancy men and women there dancing around and in slow motion like machines in a factory. Chris couldn't comprehend how unbelievably lucky and unlucky he was at the same time.

The men stood in front of him, and he waited for a long time until she came through again and didn't look at him, pushing through the crowd and grabbing her purse. She took his hand.

"Chris Stallingworth, we are going home."

He didn't feel anything less than surprised and ashamed, as he apologized to her at least a million times.

"Babe, I'm sorry, I-

She was quiet the whole way on the way home. Chris bit his lip and looked outside at the stars. They seemed fancy and decorated in the sky like the wedding cake that was worth at least a thousand dollars to get decorated and polished. A thousand-dollar cake that was gobbled in less than five minutes.

They were silent until they got back to the bedroom. He and her store in the opposite direction and were faced on opposite sides of the bed. He fiddled with his hands and then he turned around and quickly spooned her and kissed her back.

"Look, we are married now, let's try to remember all of the amazing things we've done."

A tear fell from her eye and she fell deeper into her grasp. They fell asleep comfortably and Chris realized he would never love another woman like this one.

He wanted to cry and never let her go, as her body fit into his like a lock and key. He never wanted another fight, another power clash, another struggle. He wanted his honeymoon to last like this forever.

Chris thought about that night as the struggles would pile up, but at that moment, he felt safe with her, like he was meant to be with her forever.

That's when he would face the inevitable future with his wife: divorce.

Chapter 6:

Chris woke up a little later than his wife did. She was up looking out the window, getting dressed to leave. He put his clothes on. His father-in-law bought him a nice collared shirt and fancy jeans, and he walked to the bathroom and shaved some of his stubble. She was still looking out the window.

The weather was a bit rainy that morning, as the island was eventually getting lonelier and lonelier. The forever summer that existed was temporarily dark and gloomy.

He looked at his wife and then shook his head, sitting at the edge of the bed. He washed his face again, trying to wipe off the poison that was still in his pores and he got some of the water on the shirt. He looked at himself again, her still being silent. He wanted more than anything to kiss her and tell her it would be alright, but she was just silent. There were no words for the terror that he caused, and he acted like he didn't do anything.

He came back out, and she looked at him longingly, getting up and giving him a slight kiss, and walked away to get dressed.

He stood in stunned silence, and he wanted more to turn on the television and distract himself with some politics or whatever war was going on in other countries. He wanted to drink more. He wanted to escape the wealthy parts, the superficial, the very things that his parents were proud of, he wanted to take a boat to another island and never come back.

Chris Stallingworth wasn't an incredibly built man. He had one tattoo and he had a nice jawline and looked older than his age, but he was not all the politician was, the once crew cut, the handshakes, the government politics, the staunch and impressive nature that he possessed, the lack of diversity that Chris's town possessed. The workers, the kids who liked the art in these cities he worked in, the kids who expressed themselves through the paintings and the graffiti that spread through the towns were like fresh reminders of a life outside the cookie-cutter lifestyle he found himself in. He liked art and expression deeply, but he was scared of life outside his place.

The sex. That is what kept him there. The sex was melodic, like music that kept him going. He wanted every inch of her, he wanted to sing songs that he could never sing, and he wanted to give himself some time to process everything that she was doing. But he never imagined a suffering marriage that was so quick to leave his sight. He was nothing but a beta male in the race of survival to the top.

"C'mon baby, we need to leave soon." His wife said quickly and sternly as she applied her makeup and Chris got up and looked at her. She was simply beautiful, but not in the way that the forest girls were, but in her way. His friend that hosted her had rugged and curly hair, but his wife's hair was straight and preened, and he could not imagine such a contrast.

He bit his lip because she was looking beautiful and his mind didn't want to say something was missing, but it was. He was lost for words as his gorgeous wife took her fancy bags and they both left in silence.

They both sat on the airplane, also in silence. She then nudged him and told him that her father was waiting for them.

When they got to the gate, the politician was there with the bodyguards and looking at Chris very visibly disappointed, and looking at his daughter with disgust. Chris for some reason wanted to shout at this man and say that another man was hitting on his wife and he did not approve, his head was spinning with anger, but the politician put his hand in front of Chris, and motioned his daughter to come to him.

"Chris, give us a moment please."

Chris stopped and looked around at the atrocity. His father-in-law treated his daughter like a little girl.

He wanted to shout, as his tension was increasing and increasing, but there he stood dumbfounded at his lack of luck with his father-in-law like this man wasn't family but a mere soldier standing in between him and his wife.

He clenched his fist and felt the tension escalate through his body like a snake would swirl around in muddy water. He stood there again, looking deep into his wife's eyes as she looked back slightly, smiling tensely, but then didn't say anything to her father. She walked back to Chris and patted his shoulder.

"Sorry about that, we should go."

"What was that about?" He asked her, as sweet as possible despite his inner rage.

"Oh nothing, he wanted to congratulate us on our honeymoon."

Chris stopped in silence and for the first time he seemed completely distant from his wife, despite wearing the fancy cologne, the fancy shirt, the pants, he seemed completely alien in this strange world. The cameras weren't there for the first time and the spotlight was completely gone.

He never knew about her like this in college. He was actually at a somewhat prestigious college like his father asked him that one day. That was mostly due to his father's proverbial nudging that he apply to that college, and Chris did at one point feel that he wasn't good enough for it, as he liked the drink and being with the boys, relaxed and in nature, but he was here. They met and he had no idea that this was the family. This was the senator, the main politician, the man who had total control of his daughter, her whereabouts, her interests, her everything. He was watching her, and he had total control.

Chris thought about the wilderness, and the days he spent there, camping out there. The birds were around, and he remembered deeply and disturbingly a hawk capturing two of the birds in the sky, its talons biting deep into its flesh, and the screams that the birds had. He remembered the image deep in his mind, the poor birds were innocent, incapable of ever doing anything wrong, yet it was strangled, matted, and taken away for the other birds to eat.

He thought about the days again in the woods, the crisp smells of fall, and the apples they picked were fresh and sweet. He would go out with his buddies and they would laugh about the sports in the town and they would talk about how annoying the bugs were. They were about the stars, and Chris liked the birds. He loved the cardinals, as the youthful days were upon them. He noticed their red wings and their handsomeness. How nature never worried about other birds or other people or other hawks. It was just him and his ladybird, getting the seeds on the ground. If the hawk got them though, the hawk got them. It was the hierarchy. It was the circle of life.

He didn't like the hawks, how they wrestled around in the sky, the sun beating down on their wings, and how they circled, watching every move that the little birds made.

Chris's town was large, or large enough where they had spirit and the differences were almost apparent, but not too common. There were all sorts of people, all sorts of things to discuss. He felt at home, like a part of a greater whole.

The politician watched Chris with piercing eyes as Chris went away with his wife. He felt the shirt get sweaty and then scratchy, as she fell into his arm, and subtly noticed that he was sweaty but she didn't care enough as she leaned against him forcibly. He put his arm around her in a caring way and shot her father a quick look, enough to engage, but not enough to be threatening.

They remained in silence as they got home. Chris went to work the next day.

He was sobbing as he was in the car with his father remembering the memory, as they drove home, the house he and his wife lived in was unprotected.

He remembered how exciting he and his wife were when they bought the home. They were just newly engaged and Chris's buddies commented on how he was the "happiest" they've ever seen him. Chris looked into his new wife with admiration in his eyes and he held her close as they looked upon a beautiful two-story, two-bedroom home, right near the politician's mansion about five miles away.

"Babe? You ready for this?" Chris looked deep into her eyes, and her eyes shone, but not as keenly as before.

"I am more than ready." She said leaning against him.

They went inside the house. It was squeaky clean, with boxes lined up in a row on each side. The sale was not horrible and Chris was able to make a downpayment easily after working for so many years. It was his time. It was *their* time.

The floors of the house were pristine white. Chris remembers that clearly. *He and his wife,* he thought smugly, would *be getting the cleanest house that ever existed.*

Chris's father was shocked at how the house appeared to have been so pristine, like teeth cleaning and whitening from a top dentist. Chris sent him pictures and both his parents were amazed at them. Chris's wife would kiss his cheek and tell him how happy she was that they were right near her father.

"This is great, yeah." He said slowly. "I am really happy, aren't you?"

"Yes, of course." She said.

That night they got most of the things out, and Chris was tired, as he flopped his entire back on the bed.

"So, what are we naming our kids?" He asked her slowly.

She stopped for a moment, as he asked it too soon, too quickly, too abruptly her face turned pale.

"Chris, we still have to move these boxes."

He shook his head. "Of course."

They slept together that night snugly and happily. Chris knew that this would be his future and he was happy about it. He was clean-shaven, had the newest cologne, and he had a new job. He was all set.

His wife also had a new job.

As they were in bed that night, suddenly his wife got a call. It was the politician.

"Babe, we're in bed, we need to sleep." Chris rubbed his eyes groggily and then tried to fall back asleep.

"It'll only be a few seconds." His wife got up and quickly went downstairs, almost to avoid her husband completely. He leaned over in the bed and breathed deeply.

She came back after ten minutes of him tossing and turning. He saw images of their honeymoon, all of the men coming for him, and all the words continued to haunt him.

You're a girl, Chris.

He stopped breathing again deeply.

"Are you okay?" His wife asked him if he was a foreign stranger.

He shook his head for a moment and went to the bathroom and washed his face. He looked at the mirror. Clean-shaven, his eyes sharp, a new shirt to sleep in, a new life. Yet he felt like something was off.

"I'm fine." He responded promptly and then went back to bed. They cuddled for a while.

"You know it's okay to tell me what's going on." His wife told him.

He got frustrated by that comment.

"I'm fine." He pouted, turning over to the other side.

I can't believe she said that. He said in his head. *Does she think I'm a girl?*

She came up behind him and wrapped her arms around him.

"It's okay."

They slept like that for most of the first night, while Chris was hugging an invisible pillow, of someone that he could never have, could never own. He was not the politician, watching over their every move, their every mark, to make sure that they were up to standards. They were the ones that were in the microcosm, under duress, under pressure to perform. That night Chris didn't want to perform.

Chapter 7:

Chris remembers his first real alcoholic drink. Not one that was with friends, but a real one. One where if he was stressed out, that's what he went to.

He remembers having sex with his wife and then suddenly, she stopped. It was that week that they slept on separate sides, work was piling up and an average modern Americanistic couple was kicking in. He felt his sides burning often, and his eyes drooping in the mornings. Coffee could only do so much.

But his first drink was one that he'll remember. It was after work and then, in his fancy corporate job making phones driving a fancy car, it all of sudden occurred to him that his tire was breaking down. It was the afternoon, the day was stressful and he had not heard from his wife all day. The anxiety was kicking in.

She was going out again.

He tried calling her multiple times, but she wasn't there to save him. His clothes were getting sweaty and he felt his hair get a little more jilted. He decided to grow it out a bit during those days.

He took out his cell phone and called for service, and he felt his body go into another world. His wife was not calling him back and his work bookcase was sprawled across the road. His head was light, he checked his phone again, and just like that, he fell over on the side of the road.

***

When he woke up, the police were surrounding him, people taking pictures and it was late at night.

"You okay son?" The policeman patted his shoulder.

"Yeah w-why?" Chris got up to see people around him and it was on the news that night that a man passed out on the side of the road. No word from his wife that night.

Chris patted his pants and then got up, feeling his emotions like the whole world could see him at that moment and he had dirt all over his newly pressed clothes. He shook his head and the police officer stopped him.

"Have you been drinking?"

Chris stopped and earnestly shook his head, trying to not think about the one drink he had before.

The police officer did a couple of tests on Chris, and that's when he was arrested.

"Look. I swear. I-I didn't-

Chris was taken in a police car away from his car and that's when he heard from his wife.

"Chris? What the hell oh sorry honey my phone wasn't working!"

"Where the hell have you been?" He demanded as he was strapped to the back of the police car.

"Chris, I-I just was doing things at work?"

"That's the seventh damn time you've said that." He was practically screaming in the police car.

"Honey, I'm so sorry."

"Yeah, you should be," Chris said and hung up the phone.

The policemen were dead silent. They eyed each other like robotic people while Chris was breathing flesh, trapped in the indecent scene he had found himself in.

He eventually got to the jailhouse in about thirty minutes, and then he saw the politician with his daughter. She was there, crying, waiting for him.

She hugged him tightly, while the politician scolded him. They had the money to get him out of the DUI fine and they did just that.

Chris's hands were finally released and he stood, eying the politician. His glare was like that of a hawk's, steady and fierce, with Chris being his prey. His wife embraced him again and they left, just like nothing happened. Though he would have a hearing later about potentially losing his license as well.

That night was a night of no sleep. Nothing as Chris tossed and turned. His wife wasn't present as she slept on the other side of the bed. The alcohol started to go from Chris's breath the next night when he stopped at the liquor store that was about a few blocks away after his buddy from work drove him in. The excuse was that he was on medicine for a temporary condition.

"Babe, you want anything?" He called her on the phone.

"No, I'm good." She said slightly. "I'm surprised you are getting alcohol after what just happened. Did you learn anything from that?"

Chris coughed a little. "I don't care."

That night the smell of alcohol filled the room.

As the days went on, the pristine smell turned into a faint smell of alcohol in the earlier days of the house, and the drink was piling a little in the trash can. Chris laid back after work and drank a little as he watched his wife organize and put things away. They did not talk much when they got home and Chris turned on the television.

"Chris, honey, this is not okay." She said sternly.

"What? I want to see the local news."

"First it's the alcohol, then the local news, and then it's something else."

"Babe, I just want to know what happened in sports."

She looked at him, very sternly, almost the first time that he saw that. She was very scary to him at that moment, like a machine was looking back at him, reprimanding every action that he took. It wasn't his mother, it was his wife, the closest companion, the closest person in his life. She was the one who was supposed to be his confidant and she was acting like a robot.

Chris leaned back and took another sip of whiskey he got at the store.

"Didn't you learn anything??" She raised her voice a little.

Chris stopped and put the drink away.

"I'll be fine." He said convincingly only to himself, but she had a way to look deep into his eyes, yearning for him but having the guts to say anything would be horrible, to be honest. She knew that he was tough around the edges, but never this tough.

Chris came up and kissed his wife gently, and then put the drink down. He realized that he didn't have much contact with his family and his friends back home and he was missing them. Work was routine, and he put his suit and tie on for an electronics company with his economics and electric engineering double major degree and that's all he did, while she was in the other room focused on her earnings, doing the taxes, doing the cooking while Chris drank and dreamed of the better days. The days he was out in the woods. He looked back at his wife, and she looked back at him still longingly like in the younger days, and they came up and kissed.

"Let's go to bed?" He suggested as they both curled up together in bed.

Chapter 8:

Chris was not stopping, as he promised, as his wife was showing up less and less, and then one night the alcohol ended up on the floor, the red wine against the white tile floors.

"What the fuck Christopher?" She came home late that night with him waiting for her.

"Where the fuck you been?"

"I-I was just out."

Chris was madder and madder, the hours at work were longer and longer and when his friend drove him home the alcohol filled his mind. He was getting angrier and angrier the longer his wife stayed at her job. She would pass the days and sometimes come back home around 9 pm, or maybe 10 pm and Chris would be awake, waiting for her, for she wasn't at a night shift ever (she hated staying up late), with an alcoholic drink in his hand. He was not always running, though his weight stayed down due to his unwavering anxiety, waiting for her to come home.

If she wasn't home, the politician was calling her phone, typically in the mornings, when they would engage in their bedroom routine. That night it was different.

Chris started to act like her father, the politician once eventually she came home.

"I'll have 'er by six." He raised his voice. "By eight sir."

He walked around, pranced around. "I run the world! I know your every move. I run the world!"

"Chris, you need to calm down." She put her hands up and then Chris looked at her like he realized the power he had as the wine spilled on the floor and the beer bottle was in midair and he stopped, caught the bottle, and put it down on the counter.

It was familiar to her, absolutely, and he didn't want to admit that. He was trying to protect her but the politician's influence was everywhere, as he towered over their love, their house, which was smelling more and more like booze, the couches were more rugged and their love was strained.

Chris stopped and started sobbing. He missed his family dearly, again. His wife, unlike she normally would, walked around him and then took the alcohol can away from him. She became someone he didn't recognize, the robot look on her face, the machine that he could not take away.

"Chris, I think we need to sleep in separate rooms tonight." She said sternly.

He nodded his head.

"I've got the couch."

"Good." She nodded. "Go to bed, okay?"

She looked at him with some care in her eyes, but he looked back at her with pain, with humanity, with emotion that she did not have in her look or it was fading away slowly.

He stopped and took a deep breath and got a cover and slept deeply on the couch.

"Ben?" He called out in the night. "Ben..."

They talked about their kids, and the son that Chris would have would emulate the child that he saw at the playground. It was springtime, with the cold crisp air arising and the sun falling and the child had brown hair as he did. Chris went with his wife to a playground near his parent's house when they were young and dating. The child had a face of an angelic, angelic like the world was opening up in front of them. He slid down the slides, his laugh was infectious with his baby teeth still in. He seemed to be about three or four years old and was playing with the other children, he was like a leader to them and they followed him as he pointed to the other children to move in a certain spot. His mother called for him.

"Ben? Come here, sweetie."

Ben went over to his mother, giving her a big hug and she melted into his arms. Chris looked at his then-girlfriend and kissed her on the cheek.

She smiled. "We have to name our child Ben, you know if we ever have kids."

Chris laughed. It was the morning a few weeks before the high school reunion party.

Chris looked back at the child and thought of him, how sometimes he would go out to the soccer field and there was little Ben with his buddies out on the local soccer field, and how Chris looked deep into the child's eyes. Ben stared back at Chris and they exchanged a look, and Chris realized that in his mind, Ben was himself.

Chris woke up in the middle of the night that they slept in separate rooms, choking on his sweat and spit. The alcohol was deep and inbedded in his mouth.

"Honey-

She was nowhere to be found. The house was silent.

Chris stumbled upstairs, as he realized the smell of alcohol was getting stronger and stronger in the house, and he noticed an unfamiliar smell somewhere in her room. He went in and she wasn't there.

He panicked but in his drunken state, he called her. She answered.

"Where the hell are you?"

"C-Chris I went to see my dad."

"That fucking-

She hung up and Chris screamed at the phone. "Fuck!"

He kicked some of the alcohol cans around. "That damn senator!"

He realized that no one would be heard by his rants and he was alone for the night. He sat on the couch and took another beer out of the fridge and drank it. The alcohol was dripping down his mouth and went down his shirt until it spilled on the floor.

"Damn beer!" He shouted.

Some of the neighbors in the next house over came over to his place. They were friends of the politician.

They knocked on his door.

"Christopher? Are you okay?" They asked him outside. "You've been yelling all night, and it's very loud."

"I-I'm fine." He said, a bit shaken himself. The fact that his neighbors had the kindness to ask him kept him in his shell, he was shy again, and he opened the door, but they were not there.

He shook his head. His hair was growing out slightly since he got it cut the week before and he was feeling dizzy.

The next morning, his wife found him passed out near the front door, and the politician was with her looking down at Chris. He and even her looked like they were going to kick him even more.

"What in hell's name are you doing boy?" The politician went on his knees and eyed Chris so callously, Chris peered back with sheer stress as he turned over.

"I-I'm fine sir." He said, after missing the morning, after lounging in his pajamas, after missing work that morning, after the escape and rescue from the DUI, it would be the last time that he saw the politician again.

The politician stood up and wiped his shirt, so cleanly so profoundly, so immensely that Chris could see the nice steel shoes and the swanky look and the smirk.

"Have a good day Christopher."

He walked out leaving him with his wife.

"W-where the hell you been?"

"I think I am leaving." She said as a matter of factly.

Chris looked in shock. "What, how?"

Another man with steel shoes and a white coat came into the door, wrapping his arm around his wife. Chris was stunned.

"This is my boyfriend Chris." His wife said, and to his shock. He got up.

He almost shook the man's hand but Chris was still stunned.

The man looked at Chris with apprehension, but the politician was eying Chris like a hawk from down the stairs.

"If he starts a fight, I will call the police." The politician said to his wife, now to be ex-wife.

"We have another house, Chris." The politician said smugly. "C'mon on now."

He stopped, tears flowing down his eyes, as he held his wife's hands.

"H-how could you do this?"

She kissed his hands. "I'm sorry Chris, it got too far. My dad and I have a lawyer. He'll come by soon."

Chris looked dumbfounded as the tall man in the white coat, saying Dr. followed by the last name, caressed his wife's shoulder and kissed her head while her ex-husband was right there. *Right there in front of him.*

The doctor and his wife left him in the cold and the dust, the heat no longer working in the house, and they eyed him slowly, his wife cold towards Chris, but a tear did fall down her side.

"Bye Chris."

He reached his hand out and pulled it back, feeling the pain creep up inside of him as they left, the politician motioning them to go ahead.

He looked back at his wife and said words Chris would never forget.

"I guess only the strongest survived. You are leaving behind a saint though. A fucking saint."

He lifted his shirt, showing his tattoo. She didn't look back and they left in the car taking them to a new home.

Chapter 9

The once white house was smelling stronger and stronger of alcohol and Chris was alone. He went to the back of the house, kicking the cans, and then in stunned silence, picked them up. No more politicians, no more cuddling, no more love.

He stopped and that's when there was a knock on the door. It was hours later, and that's when the lawyer showed up. Chris was stunned, with his hair starting to jut out, and his workplace calling frantically. It was the first real-time he had missed work.

"I-I have a family emergency." He talked to his boss shaking. "My family is falling apart."

"Chris, is everything okay?" His boss seemed genuinely concerned.

"T-the lawyer is here." Chris was dumbfounded again, as he felt his head burning and the headache coming back.

"Okay, okay, take the day to cool off." His boss knew his instincts were correct. "We'll connect more tomorrow, Chris. Just hang in there, okay?"

Chris Stallingworth knew of his brilliance. He knew of his kind heart, and he wouldn't let this lawyer take the best of him.

"I am sorry, *who are you*?" He asked, shaking his head.

"I am your wife's representative. We just need to talk about your pending divorce."

"Well, I need to get my lawyer too! This is immediate don't you think?" He shrugged, sighing. "I was not prepared for this."

"It seems like this was coming for a while." He replied.

"It's her father." He responded, trying to calm himself down, as the lawyer smelled the alcohol, he almost moved away.

"Oh Chris," he patted his shoulder. "Get some help. We'll talk more tomorrow."

The lawyer shut the door promptly and Chris was left in shambles, as he cried hard on the ground, sobbing deeply and profoundly as his treasure of a wife was taken away.

He went back to the mirror. He no longer had the attractive stubble. He was no longer on the news, for the moment at least. He was no longer the center of the beautiful girl's life. He didn't know what "better" meant. Like he was already damaged. Like his life had come to a roaring halt and he didn't have anything else to look forward to.

He sighed and looked at the alcohol that was keeping him company. She was the real bride in the relationship, the queen of his heart, and she swept him away. While his wife was off with a doctor, he was off with his new affair with alcohol.

He kissed the cap so passionately, imagining it was his wife, and he moved around the room like he was dancing with her, so magical, so intensely, he thought he was with her. He moved with the motion of the wind, and he felt the side of the beer can as he danced for the next hour.

He sat down on his couch and cried slowly and surely, the reality was hitting him hard. She would never come back. His luxury, his lover, his playmate, everything, the normalcy, and the way his friends talked about their wives never occurred to him that he would lose his.

Her perfume wafted in the room and he felt a small scent. It was lavender scented, and she wore it to help him sleep. Everything she had everyone wanted, and he knew that. He was trying to rationalize it like his dad rationalizes the Pythagorean theorem.

He counted to ten in his mind. Then he stopped and took a breath. The moments were slowly slipping away from him and he just stared ahead. There was no light in the house, the bottles were piling up on the sides of the kitchen, the couch was worn from him sleeping there the night before, the pillows falling within themselves, and his whole identity was falling apart.

He poured some alcohol on himself once he got in the kitchen against the black shirt he slept in, like he was Jesus Christ himself, he went back up and took off his spilled alcoholic shirt and put it away to be washed. It wouldn't be washed, but he looked at it, noticing the red wine staining it, presumably like the blood from the lamb had stained Jesus's pure and perfect life.

Chris was religious. He loved Christ and loved Jesus and church when he was younger. He went with his father and he was pure Christian. He sang in Church. He vowed to marry a very pretty and wealthy woman and treat her well. He was happy in those days with his family surrounding him. It was cheery and bright, and the sky was yellow and orange with hope and light.

Chris thought that his life would be perfect like it was in church. Nobody yelled at anyone. There weren't fights. There wasn't anybody trying to take over or destroy anyone's happiness. It was safe in the woods in his town. But once they got out, there were the typical booze-filled nights, the families trying to shelter the children from going to parties and in the city, the parents silently doing things behind closed doors. But the light in that church was where Chris would go after his wife left and him bending his knees on the floor was all he knew how to do.

Chris wept on his knees, praying to some God that he would be set free. From whatever it was: alcohol addiction, his wife's life, whatever it was, he prayed. He didn't often do that and didn't want to do it, but he was becoming slower, slower, more and more desperate as he started to get up. He looked at the bottle like his wife was back. He shook his head.

He went into the other room and turned on the television. He plopped himself on the couch. He watched a small man outside of a bar. He was stout, proper, and laughing, engaging with the camera about a new bar that had been built in the honor of someone that Chris didn't know and didn't frankly care about. But he knew that he should go there. For whatever reason. He wanted to pick up some pretty girl and call her his for the night. It wasn't religious, by any means. He was not religious at that moment, but he was hoping that God would forgive him in some capacity eventually.

His dad promised to play chess with Chris the next day that he would come back to the house and repeat their calm and cool days in the house. The sweet breeze would come over them. Chris remembers one day he was playing chess and he was about to win.

His dad smiled deeply at his son. "You aren't going to do that aren't you?'

"Do what?" Chris smiled back, laughing. "You can't possibly realize that?"

"I did see it and it's brilliant." His dad chuckled, a rare angelic moment that Chris remembers. It was right before he got married, the rare days he was alone with his father.

"I am, yes, I am sacrificing the queen to checkmate you daddy boi." He laughed and proceeded to move.

A few minutes later, checkmate.

Chris rubbed his head at that moment, wondering if his mental capacity would ever stand the test of that time.

It was at that moment that he realized his sacrificial move was exactly what he needed to win. To understand himself. To understand the purpose of his life.

He got up. He went to the bathroom and shaved a little bit of his stubble but his hair was a mess still.

"Baby, baby. I am gonna get you back." He whispered as he buttoned one of the shirts the politician gave him for his birthday many years ago.

"Gonna get you back."

He looked like his old self, minus the crazy hair, as he sat there and sighed and then cried a little, some numb tears that were falling like he didn't even recognize it. He stumbled out, as he realized he kept some of his stubble around the beard area, tears streaming down his face, as he walked outside and hugged one of the trees nearby. It reminded him of home, of his father, and the chess games they were going to play.

Then he passed out for the day. When he woke up, he was determined to find a girl. He, with his fists clenched, went out to the bar. He walked there since it wasn't too far away. He shook his head in the rain that was pouring down his leather jacket that his father got him years ago that Chris liked and his golf polo that the politician got him. He stepped into the bar in the city, and there was a girl. A dark-haired girl that looked somewhat like his ex-wife, just not nearly as beautiful.

"Hey, pretty lady-

At that moment, he was dragged out in the open.

"That's my mother fucking girlfriend ya hear?" A man with tattoos yelled at him as two thugs approached him.

"Get this twig ass man."

Two men nearby yelled and all Chris could see were newscasters and his dragged face out in the open.

"Ben?" The reporter asked.

"I'm s-sorry." He stuttered. "Not Ben. It's C-Chris. Chris Stallingworth." He said to the cameras.

Chapter 10

After being on the news, Chris's meeting with his lawyer was not as expected. His wife's lawyer was technically going to be ousted by this one, hopefully, and this one seemed nicer on the phone, so Chris tried his best. He cleaned the cans on the floor and sprayed the floors with a cologne that would disguise the alcohol smell. Since he didn't have his license after the hearing that happened a while ago that Chris didn't fight, the lawyer offered to come to him. He was completely shaved at this point, his hair still bushy, but his stubble was completely gone, as he tried to look put together but the bags under his eyes were still prominent. At least his hair was also combed over. His lawyer stared at him, clearly worried about his mental health, but keeping professionalism was his priority. In his nice blue suit and tie, he walked up to Chris in the house before Chris's dad took him away and the house would be sold eventually, where his wife would never come back to him again.

"So Chris? Chris Stallingworth?"

"Yes?" He lifted his head, as drearily as he lifted his chin exposing some of the markings the men made on him the night before.

"What are you doing up this early? You look exhausted?" The lawyer showed some genuine concern, but then his eyes shifted to a more sinister look.

"Why did you get beat up? What did you do to get to this point?"

Chris looked back at him, with some fury and some rage. This man appeared so robotic, so subtly in charge of his destiny, where Chris knew that he wouldn't win the irreparable damage that his ex-wife put on him. He would figure out what to do with the settlements, and what to do with the house, and the fact he would live with his parents was even more numbing for his future. His job was constantly calling and he had no answer for them.

Chris wanted to cry but he looked the lawyer straight in the face. "She was my stability, my partner in crime. And she left me. She fucking left me."

The lawyer was taken back by that answer and decided to take a few steps back.

"Maybe now is not a good time."

"Maybe never is a good time." Chris shot back, as he wiped a tear away. "Never."

The lawyer sighed. "We have to do this eventually."

"When? When will she realize that she isn't a good person?" Chris sobbed a little and then straightened up. "Okay let's do this."

"Do you feel you're in an okay place to do this Chris?" The lawyer said as his shoulders propped up and he asserted his dominance in a way that made Chris extremely angry.

"When would be a good time, Mr. Lawyer?" Chris sneered and got up, going to get water from their semi-operational refrigerator.

"Okay, Chris." The lawyer stopped Chris from moving. "I am your lawyer, I am trying to settle this dispute. I am going to defend you."

Chris shook his head. "When have you defended anyone in your life?"

"Your father hired me."

Chris stopped for a moment. Then he turned around. "My fucking father hired *you*?"

The lawyer stopped in his tracks. "We are trying to help you, Chris, through this difficult time."

Chris sighed and staggered over to look at the papers.

The lawyer was increasingly concerned but then patted Chris's shoulder. "There, there."

Chris looked up at him and laughed. "You think that will make me feel better?"

The lawyer laughed subtly and then said. "Look, we need to focus."

Chris smiled for the first time in a while and then looked at the notes. He noticed that the other lawyer wasn't coming and an "x" was next to his name.

"What did you do to my ex-wife's lawyer? Murder him?"

Chris's lawyer laughed.

"No, he was a slight bully behind closed doors, to be honest." In his monotone voice, he continued. "We tried to get him to leave you alone, but you had some influence in his decision. He was too proper, to be honest. He was going to harass you more and more, to be honest about the house. And the DUI and maybe do some criminal charges...so it's in his best interest to leave you alone if there's going to be a more peaceful dispute."

Then the lawyer turned to Chris and gave him more of a sad look. "The house we are going to fight for so you will stay here if you want to. But I don't know what you'll do with the DUI. That makes this harder also to keep the house since there is some legality in that. Maybe you can continue to carpool."

"That would be great, to be honest," Chris muttered and then sat down.

"It's a good thing you didn't have kids. Custody battles are much harder and stressful." The lawyer said.

"If we did, I would have had Ben." Then Chris started to tear up a little. "Ben."

"Oh." The lawyer connected the dots. "There, there. It's okay."

Chris hugged the lawyer and to his human dismay, the lawyer hugged back.

"This is such an organic moment, you know between us?"

Chris laughed a little in his tears. "Don't get that way with me please?"

"I understand your pain." The lawyer launched back. "My wife and I haven't always had an easy road either."

Chris stopped for a moment, appreciating this man's humility and humanity, realizing that maybe humans have this innate desire to fit in with the crowd. Wear the nicest ties. Say the nicest things. Love the nicest people. But when it gets down to it, they aren't the nicest things. They aren't the nicest ties, they aren't the nicest people. And that to Chris's realization is when humanity shows. When the truth is exposed, the light can start coming to fruition.

Chris felt the tattoo on his waist. He got it when he was very young. He realized that maybe somewhere there wasn't the faintest idea why he saw this, but what did it mean to be the strongest? He pondered as the lawyer penned a few things and Chris subtly touched his knee.

"Lawyer, can I ask you something?"

"Anything." He promptly replied, a little taken back by the touch.

"Why are you stronger than me?"

The lawyer laughed a little, knowing what Chris meant.

"Sometimes the strongest aren't always what they seem to be." He replied, patting Chris on the knee back.

Chris was taken aback by the touch, but this man was still human. Chris's eyes were set on him and then he thought about his wife and how he acted.

"Damn, I gotta get her back." He went up and tried to leave the room, but the lawyer stopped him.

"Chris? What are you doing?"

Then Chris cried into his suit, trying not to ruin it, but temporarily he cried. "I ruined it Mr. Lawyer. I ruined it all. With my selfishness and pain. I used alcohol to cover it. I ruined it. It ruined it all."

Chapter 11

"Chris?"

It was his father on the other line.

"Chris, you okay?"

Chris was sleeping in and groggily answered the phone. He hadn't answered the lawyer that his dad hired and his dad's calls were going to voicemail. He hadn't been at work for a couple of days at this point, but slowly he was going to get back there.

He had slept most of the day, with the rooms continuing to reek with alcohol. He got up this morning, however, and cleaned the rooms. He stopped and looked at pictures of him and his ex-wife. The trips to the tropics, the wedding, how happy he looked holding her. The typical American dream.

He turned them over and sighed. He felt physically sick. He felt like he wasn't able to stay awake during the day and he thought of her at night. He couldn't possibly work without her by his side. He would cry or sleep during the day and then drift into a deep depression around nighttime.

He remembered how music changed his mind about things. He tried it, going to a local store and buying some headphones and started to listen to strings and then more modern music about breakups. He resonated well with it, and he began to relax at night. This was the night before his dad came and got him and they went back home. Back to his parent's house.

He didn't want to think about the death of the house at that moment. It was the music, the sweet music that kept him thinking about her, and he was crying but staying stable.

He wasn't angry. He wasn't upset. He didn't want to drink. He just lied there, in contention wondering about all the parts about depression, a foreign entity to him at this point.

Depression wasn't something that was set in stone. It came in waves for Chris. One day that week he couldn't manage to get out of bed. On this day, walking outside was fine. It was a couple of days after the bar fight and still, he was having PTSD from that. The men, the massive men dragging him out. He probably still had a few scars from that. Emotional and physical.

He stopped and breathed heavily and then got a vape. He tried it, smoking was somewhat helpful, but he found drinking was heavily helpful. But he stopped that day, in his tan coat and shaggy hair and a now developing stubble, he put the drinks away. The house wasn't by any means clean, but it was getting better. His wife hadn't mentioned anything about the house, so it was his at the moment, and thankfully, he could sell it in his own time.

He wanted deeply to burn the place to the ground. When he lit the therapy candles his wife liked, that's what he thought. He went out and grabbed food when he could. He just tried to not think about his existence and his body and mind were in another setting. All he could picture was that little kid Ben with his mother at the playground or leading the kids on the soccer field.

Chris sat down in his silence. It was the silence that was the hardest part. He could hear her laugh and her kissing him. It was those deep moments that he felt. The anger had subsided. The lawyer had hugged him back. Now it was just the moments, the memories. The sadistic motions from the politician made him cry, not get angry anymore, just cry.

It was grief that pained him. It was days of sleeping for hours on hours and the job calls. Eventually, it was his dad calling and calling. He couldn't stay here anymore. He knew that.

"Dad?" He answered suddenly.

"What do you want?"

"We're coming to get you, Chris." He said with a very solemn tone in his voice. "You shouldn't have to stay in that house."

"Dad, please." He said, softly. "This is my home."

"It's not home if you're not happy there." His dad replied.

Chris hung up the phone and didn't answer any other calls from his father, which were many.

Chapter 12:

That night Chris wasn't expecting his father, but he came. His father didn't have any other moment and the drive was a long way to the house. Chris looked back at the once squeaky clean house. He packed a bag and thrust it into the back. It would be one of the last times he went back to the house.

His dad was silent, with no words. It was the first time that he ever was like that. He was a talker, and this time there was just nothing. Not even a pin drop could be heard. Chris tried to start talking but his father's eyes were on the road, no word, no sound.

Chris went back and looked outside. He sighed and fell asleep in the car.

Sleep was a common thing later. Chris would crash on his parent's couch like he was when he was younger after a wrestling competition or baseball competition and his youthful past was coming back to him. But he had no wife.

The depression filled his mind suddenly like a volcano that would never really erupt. He stayed down on the couch for hours that day, despite his father asking to play chess with him, he ignored everything until his dad shook him.

"Christopher, you've got to get out of this."

Chris sighed and turned his back over. The nice lawyer agreed to a long drive and was supposed to come over in a few hours, but Chris didn't want to deal with it. It reminded him of her.

He dreamed of them together on the ocean, but only a piece of her hand was holding him while her body was detached. Then he saw the politician laughing as his daughter was now completely detached and her handsome husband walked away while they were laughing and Chris stopped in the sand on his knees crying out to something, whether that was God or some other entity, he didn't know what. But she was no longer there.

Chris woke up an hour later not knowing where he was. His dad was there looking at him sternly.

"Chris? What are you doing?"

"Dad, I-

The door knocked. They guessed that the lawyer was going to be there earlier than expected.

"Christopher." His dad nodded.

Chris almost laughed to himself, as he realized the crazy mental breakdown he had with this very lawyer almost a few days ago. He opened the door, and the lawyer still looked as stoic as ever, like the hug didn't make a difference, though his voice then softened, and looked deeply into Chris's eyes as he started to slightly relax.

"Chris."

"It's good to see you again, Mr. Lawyer," Chris said in embarrassment as he was still in his faded jeans and shirt that he wore on the couch.

The lawyer sat down on the couch of the modest home and talked to him.

"We have had a settlement. Unfortunately, the house won't be in your possession."

"What?" Chris shot a look at his father, who also looked shocked.

"Look, that house should be his? What is that bastard politician doing now?" Chris's father sneered. "I never liked that bastard."

"But you get half of the profit." The lawyer said, ignoring the insults that were flung in a very deserving way. "It was the best I could do. They were threatening much deeper consequences."

Chris laughed at himself, realizing the healing process. "It was my fault to marry this woman."

Chris's dad shot a glance in his way, in somewhat shock.

"You loved her Christopher."

Chris got up and wiped a tear away. "I did, Dad I did. But for someone who *loves me* doesn't *cause this amount of pain.*"

Chris walked up and got a glass of water. "What's next Mr. Lawyer?"

"How's your job going?" He responded.

"Oh, my job-

"He'll get back to it, but it's far away. Shit." His father shot him a glance. "Chris, what the hell are you going to do?"

"Get a job here."

"Chris, it's so barren here- do you think you can find a good engineering job here?"

"I'll try."

Chris laid back down on the couch. "Hit me, lawyer."

"That's all I had to say. And you can go to the court and fight it."

"I can't fight this," Chris said. "I don't want to see her again."

Chris's dad looked at him in shock and then the lawyer. "There's not an official trial?"

"Not officially, but Chris can fight it."

"Fight for the house, Chris."

Chris got up. "Let's settle for half. I don't need to go to a fucking trial."

He got up to write some in his old journal and left the lawyer and father in shock, while the divorce papers would be signed at another time. Chris would never see the lawyer again after the signature that happened a week later with lots of loss of sleep and crying in between.

Chapter 13:

Chris got a check in the mail for about half the profit. It was a good start if he was going to move forward. He called his job and left, but soon he had a new job.

He sat in a new suit and started making electronic products for a local hospital, which was about an hour away from his home. His dad offered to take him while he was getting his license back, which was going to be soon enough.

He got up in the morning and spoke to the interviewer related to the job.

"No way, I'm sorry about your divorce."

"It honestly made me much stronger," Chris noted, no longer drinking much and keeping his focus.

His father and he played chess for the first time in a long time.

"Again, with the queen." His father laughed solemnly. "Why do you do that?"

"Sacrifice the greatest part of you and you find yourself," Chris said as his father put his kind emphatically on the edge of the board.

"Can't believe you got so good at this game, should play at the local community center."

Chris got up, with a look in his eye. "Who do you think I am? 60?"

Chris huffed and got his clothes on and decided to go for a walk.

It was about springtime, and he walked far enough to a part of the neighborhood he didn't know much about, near a newly planted garden. It was a weekend and a little chilly. He saw the gardener, an older woman. She gave him a confused look, but he had not seen a more beautiful garden. It was filled with beautiful reds, yellows, purples, and oranges. He nodded to her.

"Beautiful garden." He said to her with his pockets in his jacket.

She laughed slightly. "This winter was brutal to the flowers, to be honest."

Chris for the first time in a long time laughed to himself. "No kidding."

He hadn't noticed but his hometown did have a plentiful amount of snow. It would come especially in the higher altitudes and his hometown was a redneck sort of concoction. It was a beautiful place though with flowers like the garden. He wasn't surprised at all that he saw something like that.

He smelled the flowers. He took in every sense that he could. While the weather was a little cool, it was about that time that the spring would rise, and in his little town that was everything. He shook his head a little bit. The jutted hair was more smooth against his body, but he still felt a certain sadness. Like the type of sadness that pangs but then numbs. He was feeling it when he was walking, as the sun arose from the mountains in his small town. He was getting close to his late 30s now, close to 37 actually, and coming back to his hometown was surreal for him. His life was solely dependent on the politician and his daughter and now he was somewhat free.

But the pain continued in his heart. It still lingered. It was like a soft blow to the chest, the one where the wave of pain was lessened and lessened, like a small fighter was punching him now and he continued to feel it but he was better. The days were like that and he was thankful that his dad was there for him but still he was cut off from society.

He was like an outcast now, believing that he couldn't fit into the rigid standards that his little society put on him.

He thought about that when he walked across the barren rock paths. Something bothered him about the woods. There seemed to be an ominous quiet that surrounded it. He shook his head and moved forward into it anyways.

The trees were dark and he was consumed with the air. The sunset was close upon him. Some kids would come out here and play with things. Things he didn't know about. He remembered camping out here with his buddies. Most of them were grown with families and kids and good-paying jobs and here Chris was in the beauty of the forest. He breathed in quickly and faintly and then decided to go back.

As he emerged from the forest, he continued until he walked home, thinking of the spring flowers that he saw on his walk there.

Chapter 14:

Chris resumed his new job at a hospital near him that worked with electronics. It was a new company and was perfect for his resume. His Dad was also pleasant on the car rides. His license would eventually come back, and they went back to the town that issued his license. Chris went with his father and mother to get a new car since the politician took ownership of the old one.

At night though, he resumed his sadness. He held pillows close to him, thinking of his wife as she had died. The divorce was finalized and he never would hold her sweet-scented body. Instead, he was like a college kid, back with his parents for the summer.

He woke up, sometimes robotically, sometimes not, describing the product that he made every day. Its properties, its interconnections, its complex nature. Chris thought he was a lot like the electronics, complex and imaginary and filled with powerful motivations, but also more energized than other things. Plus, he was at a hospital and didn't want to think about his wife being there too, the irony is that that was the only place he could find a job.

He kept getting up, sometimes in the middle of the night and would remember that his wife was not there anymore. He never wanted to go to the doctors, thinking of the tall black-haired man that stole his wife away from him. The doctor's fancy black car was shiny and clean and squeaky like he had lived a good life. So lavish but so robotic. It was the robotic sense that scared Chris deeply. Because he could never be that way. Even if he tried.

There were days though when he thought about them cuddling up the same way that they did and it made him angry. So furious. Some days he was tempted to go out. And one night he did.

It was in the same area of that infamous night where the politician got in his way. That night he would have stuck up for her. If he did, he would have broken down his walls. Flooded the bricks with water. Used emotions as a storm. Use it as a weapon.

He sat down for a moment, put back his faded jeans, and went out.

There was a bar nearby where he lived that frequent college kids visited. He sat down and then looked over. Slyly but not obliviously another woman eyed him down and tipped her glass.

"Hey honey, how are you doing out here?"

He looked back slyly and hit his glass against hers. "Just getting over a divorce."

She laughed, as she was smoking the night before, but she was young enough for Chris but also not too old, and she had a pink jacket on and black hair. She winked and took his hand, her voice raspy from the smoke. Chris was slightly intoxicated but he kept his composure.

"Whatcha doin honey?" He asked as he continued to drink and drink more and more until his eyes were about to droop.

"Who's the motherfucker who dropped a dime like you?" She whispered in his ear.

Some people were staring at them as if their parents would shield their eyes from this scene, but Chris didn't think of it. He stared her down like she was a piece of steak and ate every piece like he was a starving wolf in need of comfort.

"Damn." He said, as his breath was shaky. "Damn."

She laughed a little. "You haven't been out in a while honey. Wanna come back to my place?"

Chris's eyes lit up like a dog's.

"Anything you want, I'll do it." He said, laughing to himself. He got more and more drinks.

She took him in her car, which was filled with some cigarettes and some alcohol bottles. They drove to an apartment complex a few miles away and that's when they were full on. Chris found out she was on birth control. *Great. Let's proceed.*

"You're ten times better than my ex-wife." He said in between puffs. "Fucking brilliant." She laughed softly. "I got left by my ex-boyfriend too, honey, but let's keep this night between us."

They stayed up until the early morning until both of them fell asleep with Chris cuddling her like she was his wife.

Chapter 15:

"Chris, what the fuck?"

Chris looked down on his father like he was a child. "Dad-

"Did you get the motherfucker pregnant?"

"She was on birth control."

Chris looked down on himself. *Damn.*

Shakes his eyes

He was taken back to the moment that he was out and the thugs took him out. It was the yelling that he didn't hear. Just the moments that he spent with his wife reminded him of the politician smiling at his expense. His miserable expense.

"Dad!" He got up. "Stop!"

Chris almost threw the table over where they played chess. "Stop."

He started sobbing silently. "Stop."

Chapter 16:

Chris went out to the garden one weekend morning. He just felt like it. He got up at 8 am. He never got up that early unless it was a work day.

He put on some sweatpants, and some earbuds, and listened to some music. It was soft and melodic and drastic like his life changes. He thought about her less and less, though the pain was still beating in his heart, oozing out slower and slower.

Then he wondered about the house. Who would take care of that filthy thing? The place where his past and present were intertwined in one. Where he was taken back from his drinking days to the days he lost his mind with his wife. She was the one who kept him stable and on nights like that he would be stabilized by her. He was stabilized in general.

That's when he got risky. He got out of the house to see the garden.

He saw the nice woman nearby.

"Hey, I thought I would help." He said to her, with his garden gloves. His mom offered to give them to him, and he accepted them.

She laughed, even as an older woman, her laugh was almost angelic. "Christopher, right?"

He smiled. "Yes."

"Tend to the lilac bush over there." She gave him the water tool and he started to water the flowers.

"So how has your father been?" She asked him. "I haven't seen him in a while."

Chris knew the answer to that question, but he was even more slightly appalled that she had spoken to his father. That the community life was still a real thing.

"H-he's fine." He stuttered slightly and then they were quiet as they continued to tend to the garden.

"I notice you like those woods." She said to him, "Be careful of those. You could get lost in there."

Chris nodded. "I don't go there as often anymore."

She nodded back. "Good."

Chris stopped and thought about it. *Why was she saying that?*

He hadn't known much about the forest since he went as a kid. It had been a while since he went there and he didn't know much about the forest since then. It was calming to him, almost like the trees were cheering him on and the birds were the songs in his earbuds.

He thought about all the times he was out there with his buddies. So many days, so many moments. He would argue now to the younger foolish boys that appearances aren't what they look like. He would snatch the yearbook out of their hands and say "you guys. Really? You think that the hotness is what matters?"

He just loved the wind against his face.

"So what are you doing here?" He asked her politely, thinking, but trying to come up with some sort of conversation.

She stopped and thought. "My husband died a few years ago and this garden represents something that honors his death."

She turned solemn but noticed something. "Weren't you married at some point too?"

Chris chuckled softly. "Only a little while."

They both laughed a light laugh, one filled with deep dissatisfaction and painful pasts, but the air was clean for the two folks who managed to survive.

Chris planted the lilacs slowly and then noticed them. He noticed how they fought for life but they didn't necessarily push or shove. It was just the way they were.

He tried to be that flower that was sprouting up. He tried to imagine himself as a seed, just getting up from the dirt up to the surface, he realized that he was close to that surface.

"Thank you, seriously for changing my life." He said to her.

The woman held back a few tears. "You'll be fine Chris, just keep going."

Chapter 17:

Chris Stallingworth never went back to that same bar where the thugs took him out, not that he ever would, but he did end up going to another bar close to that one on some rainy spring day.

He drove there actually. He got his license back earlier. While the spring flowers were on the other side of town, he just felt like going. Not to drink, not to make out with some pretty woman that he would never see again. Just to be. Just to feel the cold air and the crisp weather. He just wanted to feel again.

It was the weekend, of course. It was a Saturday, and he never expected to see any thugs there. He never saw someone he knew, at least in the bar.

He told his father that he was going. His father looked at him skeptically, but let him go.

Chris was safe. His father brought up the notorious news story. Chris was numb to that at some point, though he did dream about it occasionally. He was thrust hard by them, and he still had the scars of the dragging. He'll never forget the policemen looking at him, sympathizing with him so much, not knowing that he was a drunkard in his past and he never really got to a point where he was sane. He was sane now, to an extent, but he still dreamt of his wife by his side. He would never see her again.

He went to the bar that day and ordered a malt beer. Something about it stung his throat, like he was no longer really in his present reality but somewhere far off as a kid again in his past. He was thanking God that he didn't have children with his ex-wife. *Thank you, God.*

Though the bartender's eyes followed him, skeptical as well, as he drank slowly. He was numb but did not wish to drink any more than he already was. He didn't want to get drunk. The memories were slowly passing by.

He wondered. So many people got divorced, so why did his divorce stick out? Why was this so devastating when so many other people had devastating divorces? He couldn't conceptualize it. His wife had been someone he loved deeply and wanted to start a family with. His naivety was real. He thought about that for some time. His naivety was real.

He sat down and pondered about the bartender. Just watching the people. Some were young irresponsible high school kids, some were older men in their 40s and 50s, loners, or with their wives. He thought about it if he made it to 50 how he and his wife would have. But then he realized, with his sense of wisdom, that she fell into the machine. That he could not have saved her. That she was already doomed. He realized that he was in a sense doomed himself, but he could not conceptualize her doom. She lost out on the meaning of life, while he was organic. He was breathing hard. And he tasted the beer but didn't want more of it.

He paid the bartender $10 and left the bar.

Chapter 18:

There were some moments Chris would never forget, but this was the most memorable of them all. Even more than the divorce itself.

Again, it was a weekend. Work was stressful and people were questioning him. He had been there long enough that he was starting to get stressed from the judgment. *Why is he single now? What happened? Did he beat his wife? What is she doing? Where is she? Why is he still single?*

He did want to yell at them, his masculinity telling him that he wanted to end them all. His coffee was too strong, and he had a nasty habit of thinking about drinking again. Either kissing the pole that was standing there pretending it was his wife or raging about throwing beer glasses. He was well enough and healed enough to not do that right? Wrong.

It was that day he got what he was paid for.

He went out. It was getting later in the night, not quite a nighttime, more dawnish per se. He went back to the forest, without telling his father. His anger was rising, and he continued his way down the path, past the spring flowers that he tended that morning with the lady, and he went upon his way.

"This fucking life sucks ass." He said under his breath.

"Fucking sucks!" He yelled into the woods as he proceeded. "Fucking sucks."

He kicked a few twigs that were in the brambles as he proceeded. He didn't care if he was dead; he wanted to go back to where his friends were. Where the hawks were settled.

Where he had no cares. Where he was young again and there were no divorces. He was safe, with his parents. No responsibilities. Just him and his life.

He went as far as he could, like a wild man. He had no one anymore. He was about to cry. His wife was off with another man. She was dead to him, literally, dead to him. There was no way that he would get her back. And the trial that he would be able to see her at? He couldn't do it.

He felt like screaming and he did.

"AHHHHH."

He fell to his knees. A few birds whistled in the wind and moved forward as they kept their song going towards the cliff that he was about to embark on.

He wasn't necessarily in a place where he wanted to end it all. He had a good job. He and his dad played routine chess. They would sit at the table, and often Chris would sacrifice his queen. Every time. Even if he lost. His dad thought he was being petty, but that's what he would do.

Chris looked into the darkness. It was approaching 9 o'clock and he had his mind focused on the cliff. That's where he saw the hawks, but that's also where his friends used to go. He wanted to make a grand entrance or a final goodbye. He was going to leave for an apartment soon.

He felt the crisp air. He was near a pond. He got out a flashlight he had in his back pocket. This was an adventure he was set on going out on.

He kept going into the abyss. It was like this: his divorce. The emptiness he felt. The cold air against his skin continued to plague him, where there was no warm body to rest beside him at night. There was no comfort, no love in his barren lifestyle. He had no woman to turn to. He had no love in his mind.

He continued even further, though the insides were screaming at him to stop. He ignored it. Every bone in his being was set on going out there, deeper and deeper in his own emotions until he was stone cold. There was nothing else to it, no other explanation for how he was feeling. How he felt was exactly how he felt.

He felt the twigs below his feet and with his flashlight turned and recognized the same spot that his dweeb of a friend warned him about divorce. It pierced his inside suddenly. *What a dweeb.*

The engulfment of the cool night was enough to startle him. Maybe he would be caught by some other burglar. Maybe some person would destroy his guts out here. He never went so far out that he couldn't come back. But at this moment, it felt like it.

He thought the worst part was the judgment. Not even the fact that he was spouseless. That he had no woman to talk to. His best friend. His number one confidant. He loved her. And that is what made this so hard. When she walked away, so did he. And he didn't want to admit that.

He thought about her face when she left him. How she was so cold at that moment, so much expectation was put on him that it was overwhelming. Now that he was depressed, he had no more bottles to drink, no more scenes to create, no more drama, as his father said, to dispel. It was just him and his lonely-ass thoughts.

He continued onward yet again, not knowing the path much at this point. It was pitch black and his flashlight only offered a sliver of hope of getting back out. He pondered if dying out here was an option, he would gladly take it.

It fell into his soul and his heart. The fact that he had nothing. I mean he had what he needed at his parents' house. He had a job. He had a career, but he was missing one thing and that was love. He was missing that deep emotion that was caressed for so many years in the eyes of his wife and was taken away from him. That is what made him the saddest.

He started to cry. Just subtly, like a little cat crying into the night after the owner hasn't been home for a while. That's how he felt honestly. Just a little bit sad, not overly pretentious, just sad.

There was honestly no reason for this. No reason for this dependency on the one he loved deeply. She was everything, from his first to his last. She was the one who accompanied him to parties, to gatherings. He and she went to that ridiculous skirt party where all he had done was stick up for her. He loved every fiber of her being. Now, he could never see it again.

That's what bothered him the most. If he could have seen her again. He could have. At the trial for the house. The papers he needed to sign. Like this was some cartoon character in a movie that was going through a horrible battle with a monster he couldn't quite overcome yet. He felt like a powerless soul, going through the motions of his life. He was in pain quite literally at that moment, the waves of grief like a tsunami and now a patient ripple, but a hard and scornful ripple.

He continued on the path, finally reaching the cliff. He knew this part well. At least well enough. He stood over the side and looked onward. The moon was present in the distance. Somewhere, he saw the birds flying by.

It was a nice distraction, at least temporarily. He was so solemn, but there was an ounce of hope as he looked onward the cliff, and was not tempted to do much else.

However, that's when he saw it- there was a flash of unrecognizable light to his left side, deep in the forest.

"Holy shit."

Chris knew what it was immediately. *A fucking fire.*

Chris saw the light coming closer and then had a rush of endorphins go to his brain. He immediately turned on the flashlight and sprinted back into the woods, fearful, and dreading his life. He had heard about fires in the past, but this was a rare one, and he didn't dare to think about anything else other than his survival.

The light was getting closer until he could hear foreseeable flames. This is when he was full-on panicking. He held the flashlight gingerly in his hand.

"God please don't let me die tonight." He said in his head as he continued to run. Then he tripped, the flashlight going out on him as he fell.

"Fuck!"

He scraped his knee hard, the fire was unwavering at this point and it was coming even closer to him, perhaps another thirty to forty feet away. He got up as fast as he could and continued to sprint, limping partly. He was getting closer to the edge of the woods. The fire was approaching. *Faster and faster and faster.*

His heart was beating faster than ever before. Faster than a baby would on his chest, feeling the excitement that he so wanted to feel with a newborn son. His Ben was such a far-off dream, something that he could now laugh at if he wasn't consumed with flames around him. That fucking dream was so organic and so real and so true to humanity that even wishing for it seemed obsolete at this point. What was he going to gain from bringing a child into the world? What would he have experienced?

The fire was raging, angry, and mad. Emotions that Chris was numbed out to at this point in his life. It was the fleeting memories of the moment of callous indifference that his wife showed him. The indifference of the politician. He could hear him whispering in his ear.

You son of a bitch Chris Stallingworth. Worth in your name? Damn be gone if that was me. I would be alive but you'll be dead. You'll be dead in a heartbeat. Just wait and see. You're the one who will die, not me. Chris Stallingworth, you're going to die.

"Fuck." He said breathlessly as the fire was continuing to approach him and the heat was real. Even the voices of the politician seemed downright fake and a lot like himself. Like he couldn't even get *that right.*

The fire, by the way, was angry and it was growing larger and he realized at that moment that it was his problem. They were larger and larger and they were vicious. They never stopped tormenting him. But perhaps this was the final straw, the final ripple in the lake that suggested that he would never be the same man again.

Chris Stallingworth, however, wasn't going to let this defeat him. Somewhere, a tiny voice told him. *You'll make it out alive.*

He pushed forward, and finally to his dismay, he reached the end of the forest. There were alarms everywhere, firefighters bustling and hustling around and the water reached the edge, just as the fire was going to touch him, only about ten feet away, someone blew the water on the edge.

I am safe.

He fell to the ground, exasperated and thinking irrational thoughts such as *my damn flashlight was lost. How the hell am I gonna pay for that? My father got me that.*

It was ridiculous that he was having such a moment. It was crazy that something like that occupied his mind when he was literally about to die.

The firefighters continued to pour into the vicinity and he was helped up. To his astonishment, it was a face he recognized.

"Chris?"

It was a woman, the same woman who housed his wife so many years ago. She was nothing like she was before, locks of beautiful hair streamed down her dirty-looking face and she noticed his pain immediately.

"Chris."

Rubbed his eyes

"Yes, it's me. Chris Stallingworth."

She looked at him like he was dead, with so much care in her eyes. She hugged him.

"I am so sorry."

She dropped her equipment and helped him to get an ambulance. That was the last of that moment.

Once Chris woke up surrounded by his family, his dad wasn't angry. Not like a politician would be, but he was worried. His mom was there too. And the woman, the same girl that housed his wife. She was also there.

"What the hell?" He said as he slowly got up.

The doctor came in and talked briefly to his parents.

"Hey, Chris buddy, what's up?"

"Hey." He felt a bandage on his side. "Damn what did I do?"

"Were you drinking?"

"I was not, doctor."

His dad raised an eyebrow, albeit a somewhat angry one, but subtle, as if he did not want to spend his retirement dealing with another news segment on Chris Stallingworth in an ablaze fire.

The doctor patted his shoulder. "I know that you're going through a tough time, sir."

Chris noticed him and nodded. "Yes, doctor."

The doctor proceeded to give him painkillers and he rested. His mom softly brushed his hair and told him that he had a few bruises but may have almost broken his ribs in the fall he took.

He almost laughed at himself. *What a fucking fall.*

Chris eventually got up and the female firefighter and old friend went to his side.

"Chris, I am so sorry." She said about the millionth time.

She did look stunning. With soft brown hair, her face was fox-like, not quite how he remembered it, and her green eyes were shining, not like he remembered either. She looked girly, and she looked beautiful.

His masculine side was raging like a teenager. *She looks hot, what the fuck.*

He never imagined seeing her again, but her kindness back then had transcended so far that here she was, by his side again, in another unusual way, but had drastically changed. So much that her eyes were deep green like his and her voice was angelic and soft. Nothing like the hardness of his ex-wife.

"Guess what," She whispered in his ear. "I am divorced too."

Chapter 19

It was again a beautiful day, not in a tropical area, but an admittedly pleasant area. Chris has dressed in a suit again, laughing as some of his high school buddies came for this one. It was in an area somewhat close to home near a beach that Chris and his parents used to go to when he was a kid. And he had a full-on beard this time.

The mood was very light, and the days were shorter and shorter, as Chris learned to appreciate every moment. The ring bear and flower girl were on her side, as they were her niece and nephew, and he only really had his parents. But, there was a surprise.

The woman with the flowers, who barely escaped the fire too, was there, with a deep and proud smile.

That's what was also on the news as that replaced Chris's infamous run-in at the bar with the thugs. But that was all forgotten now. He was standing here, with a beautiful woman and his hands were intertwined in hers. It was about a year from that time he was caught in the flames, and his numbness faded with her touches. Her kisses, and her love.

"Can you believe this?" She looked at him, laughing so hard and so softly like he was missing something the whole time. He smiled, he smiled.

He laughed. "Well, you got hot. Like the fire."

She laughed a deep and soulful laugh like he had heard music in his ears. Never in a million years would he have imagined this woman, who had hair that was barely combed, to be standing next to him in glitter and prose as she had at that moment.

Her whole family became like Chris's family, as they instantly talked to him, the loneliness dissipated and he smiled, chatting with his wine glass and his normal talk.

"Sooooo," his new wife's mother said to him. "We hear that we're expecting a little someone in the future?"

Chris smiled and nodded. "Yes, a little boy."

"What are you going to name him?"

He turned as his wife accompanied him. He held her shoulder softly.

"We're naming him Ben." They both said in unison.

The mother, and rather not Chris, was crying.

"What a beautiful name."

Ben did come, a few months later. His voice and his cry were remembered by Chris as he started crying holding him.

You're such a girl-

No. He said, and the tears fell. *It's okay.*

He then lifted his shirt and smiled as he put the baby in his wife's arms to be held.

Chapter 20:

Somewhere, far far away, there was a crazy scene on the news. News broke out that a doctor and his wife had died in a car crash. The father was a famous senator and he was the one who could not look reporters in the face.

He broke down crying, remembering the adage.

Only the strongest survived.

A short glossary of terms, just in case:

Ph.D.- *doctoral degree*, a degree that is of the highest education level that is related to specific subjects such as math
DUI- *driving under the influence*, a legal offense that can result in what has been stated in the book
PTSD- *post-traumatic stress disorder*, a mental condition that happens after being in a traumatic experience such as physical abuse.